The Writing Box

The Writing Box

A Novel

D.J. Listort

To order additional copies of this book, contact:
Xlibris Corporation
1-888-795-4274
www.Xlibris.com
Orders@Xlibris.com
19246

For Resa

for her boundless encouragement and all her help,
and for all her strengths,
which have strengthened me

Acknowledgments

$\mathcal{F}$ew understand writing is such hard work more so than those who have within them stories which are impatiently waiting for birth from the nebulous brewing pot of inner sense and feeling to the tangible printed page.

Without assistance from the following people, it would have been extremely difficult for me to sustain the drive and the confidence needed to finish what I had started nearly four years ago.

Family and friends offered their support and encouragement, sharp insights, and biting criticisms.

I am grateful to Darilyn, Resa and Cynthia Listort, Linda Carlucci, Allison and Stephen Duffie, Tony Spada, Harold and Ingelore Stahl, Lauren Ellis, and Tom DeAngelo.

Thank you for everything.

In my heart of hearts and in my soul, I believe in the oddity of parallel lives. Although there are infinite possibilities and limitless opportunities for each of us—from the light at our birth through the darkness at our death and beyond—we do experience similar, kindred events, those strange anomalies of haphazard coincidence and curious happenstance, when the whispers of time and the shouts of circumstances, most often sounding distant and apart throughout the universe of being, come to meet, if only for fleeting moments, at the steel design of crossroad destiny.

The Afterdeath of Ethan Bishop
David Henry

1

Sunday, December 24, 2000
Manhattan

During the razor cold, blustery and flurrying late evening of Christmas Eve, a small section of cast iron water main beneath East 57th Street gradually began to flake from age, sending a slight snaking streamlet of water seeping through underground faults and chasms toward the dark basements of a small row of brownstones. Then, the main gave way. The gushing mercurial waters surged, pushing through buried nooks and crannies, reaching the foundations of the aging structures with an almost seismic force, but then momentarily were halted. Minutes later, the footings, basement walls and massive timber joists of the three abutting buildings slowly began to weaken from the constant pressure and eroding undertows of what was by then hundreds of gallons of water.

Suddenly, an underground natural gas pipe exploded below the street causing electrical lines to rupture. Spark-induced fires popped with ignition and eeled their way through the cracks in the pavement and in the sidewalks, then raced toward the buildings and caught there, quickly raging out of control.

On this holiday Eve, in apartments across the street, some families were hosting parties, others were asleep, some were beginning to unwrap presents, others were just about ready to retire for the night after setting down gifts for their children. From their windows, those who looked out could see the flames burgeoning, glowing with a slowly consuming passion in the darkness.

Alarmed and frightened, the voyeurs quickly dialed 911. The dispatchers immediately alerted the New York City Fire Department, the NYPD, and Consolidated Edison. The people watched the facades of the brownstones appear like jack-o'-lanterns, the flames relentlessly licking at the doors and window casements. The neighbors were terrified, yet intrigued by what they saw.

Then sirens blared.

On the street, a few passersby, bundled up and hunched over from the cold, watched as an EMS ambulance, a HazMat truck, four fire engines from the Engine 8 and Ladder 2 Companies from East 51st Street, two ConEd vehicles and three police cars appeared. Crusading through the mix of wind-driven snow and rapidly freezing street floods, the units seemed to come from all directions and then abruptly to stop this way and that before the burning buildings. The cars and the equipment converged like pickup sticks randomly tossed before the scene. All crews hurriedly but purposefully assembled and then divided to meet the emergency. Swirling pillars of smoke and sheets of snow helixed within the cutting winds. Hazard bars atop the police cruisers flashed and the fire engines' lights spun, strobing the darkness like blinding Christmas tree lights. Waves of heat from the now engulfed buildings blew out to the curb and beyond.

Police quickly barricaded the street. FDNY pumper crews hooked hoses to hydrants, then stationed themselves strategically for flow. Dozens of water tentacles wound about, adequately pressurized for now, but their force was weak. Ice rapidly formed as the limp sprays splashed and then crystallized. It seemed as if the buildings momentarily were being encased by the constant streams of water in thin frosty veils of opaque glass just before the heat caused the frozen mists to melt and then to refreeze, over and over again.

And then, like a dying flower, the magnificent trio of late

nineteenth century architecture slowly began to droop.

The men and women at the scene froze, but not because of the temperature. They were witnessing one of nature's most fascinating forces, gravity. The brownstones' masonry and lumber began to creak from the gradual loss of plumb. The tensile strength of the mortar, bricks, beams, rafters and joists had been compromised and now began to fade.

For an instant, the crews stood stock-still and watched, mesmerized, as the slow-motion leaning seemed to stop, then increased in speed.

"Everybody out! Now! Now! Out! Out!"

Everyone scurried for safety.

At exactly 11:25 p.m., the death came at last.

The crushing collapse sent a violent tremor through the street.

2

July 1949
Rockaway Beach, NY

$\mathcal{T}$he earliest memory I have is of nearly drowning.

I remember I had wandered off from my space where my parents had set me down on a small blanket to play with a plastic pail and shovel. I was up and about, toddling alone at the bustling water's edge, looking out at the horizon, seeing the shards of bright sunlight caroming off the wave crests, feeling the warmth of the hot summer sun on my shoulders, watching the enticing fingers of the subsiding foams beckoning me to come to play with them as they flowed out.

I remember smelling the salt-laced air, hearing the sounds of the turbulent currents mixed with the easy flip-flops of my little feet on the damp sand, the lilts of melodic voices from the scores of people and the other children enjoying that summer day.

Something soon came over me. I succumbed to that carousel of stimuli, the sinister yet pleasantly encompassing allure that was as far as my squinting eyes could see and as loud as my ears could hear.

And so, with an undefined purpose, I ran toward the outreaching water, and in that moment's breath I was falling on my way, suddenly draped over by the overwhelming surge and weight of an incoming tidal flow all about my head, the thunderous din of it as noisy as an opened kitchen cabinet filled with stacks of ceramic dishes peeling away from a wall, then crashing on the floor. I was deafened by the roaring, rumbling gurgles of undertow in my ears, unable to breathe, struggling with panic to stand, my lungs about to burst.

And then, I felt two strong hands about my waist, lifting me from my turbulent grave of darkness and salt and sand and bubbles back into the sunlight again. I was gasping for air, coughing, cold, yet burning with a fever to inhale.

Though I didn't understand the meaning of all his words then, I distinctly remember my father's distant, yet confident voice, "Now, Ursula, it's experiences like these which will help to define your character."

I've often wondered.

Did he mean that there would be times when I would be frightened, in despair, helpless, feeling like I was about to die from something dark and all around me, something mysterious, some strange forces which I could not understand and which I could not control? Or, did he mean that my destiny was to be the proverbial damsel in distress, surrendering myself in trust to a man whose physical strength and strong will would always be there to save me?

Even after all these years, I still am not sure.

Back from my watery land of the dead, wrapped in a towel and sitting on my mother's lap, I was shivering. I felt the grit of sand thick on my tongue and in between my teeth. My throat was parched from the salty water, my little heart still pumping like a diesel engine. My mind was wrenched with the knowledge of my sudden helplessness and my being at the mercy of one of nature's most tremendous forces in taking me down.

I couldn't stop shivering.

And even now, more than a few decades later, I often feel the phantom grip of my father's strong hands about my hips, rescuing me, saving me. Not quite three years old then, I came to understand the one thing which has been with me all my life.

One way or the other, there are forces everywhere which will try to control me.

3

Monday, December 25, 2000
East 57th Street, New York City

As the last of the department's equipment slowly drove away into the night, Fire Captain Thomas Angola was standing across the street from the smoldering site, leaning against the grille of his Pontiac sedan. His car's headlights, like airport beacons, pointed to the sight of the fire. Old and rusty, though dependable, Tom's Gran Prix had been a silent witness during the long hours while his men and women had worked frantically to extinguish the flames. The cold wind still gusted, making dancing wisps of the last of the smoke.

Lighting a cigarette, he stared at the small butane flame cupped in his hands. The glow highlighted his face, his straight, pointy nose, his prominent facial bones and sunken cheeks, his leathery skin and droopy eyes, each feature a testament to the opinions held by those who knew him that he was an Al Pacino look-alike. He focused his eyes on the immense pile of random bricks and charred wood.

The smell of ashes bothered him, as it always had. It was what he called the "last hurrah," the lingering essence of a catastrophe caught in his nostrils and in his lungs, that thick taste and irritating odor of carbon and charcoal that told him the fire was dead.

The streams of adrenaline which earlier had coursed and pushed through his veins were now dormant.

Most people just don't know what it's like, he thought. It's a perverse feeling when the call comes in. The anticipation, the excitement, the danger, the fright, the thought of a fiery death. It's a kind of destiny. People just don't know.

Lieutenant Anthony Vly came toward Angola, scribbling in a steno book while walking, recording observations from the night's work and noting to put in for everybody's overtime. It was nearly 1:30 a.m., ninety minutes into the next shift. The thick soles of his hip boots sloshed in the icy puddles. He also was jotting down tactical suggestions for the next "party," all of this in a lazy shorthand which only he could decipher. His angular face was blackened, his blue eyes were like ice, his hands chafed and raw from the fire and the cold.

"Look, Tom, we almost lost those two young rookies, pretty boy Myers and that broad Fernandez, when the middle one split. They both were too far inside. I kept telling them to back off, to get out. They were lucky to dodge the front wall when it came down."

Tom lost his reverie as he turned to see Vly.

"Hey, Tony, Merry Christmas," Tom said, "I thought you already went back on the pumper." He dragged again on his cigarette. Then, "Yes, Tone, I know. Fernandez knows better and so does Myers, so I think at our briefing tomorrow we've got to set them straight. With the holiday today, it'll have to wait. Still too much piss and vinegar in them, you know?"

"Right. They're just getting more and more careless, you notice?"

"Yeah, I noticed," Tom said, musing. Then, "What's the damage, Tone?"

"Look at it," he said, pointing to the scene across the street. "Total loss of the brownstones. Six injured, one of ours, Jerry D'Amato, not serious, five of them, likewise. One dead, theirs."

"Damn. Identified yet?" asked Tom.

"No. White female, between 45 and 65, apparently lived

alone. Her bags were packed. Luggage all over the place. Looks like she was going somewhere, soon, maybe tonight or tomorrow. Died in her bed. Myers carried her out."

"All right then, let's go back to the station, wrap it all up, and then it's home to the sleeping wives and kids."

The men waited a few more moments, then got in Tom's Pontiac. At ignition, the trusty V-8 roared with eagerness.

The ride back to the station was silent.

Each man was thinking about the rookie Vanessa Fernandez, and what would have to be said to her at the next briefing.

4

April 1952
Hicksville, NY

$\mathcal{I}$ was almost six years old when we moved from Bayside to Nassau County on Long Island.

I was thrilled that our new house, an unpretentious, basic cape, was couched on three sides by forests. Well, they really weren't forests, but they seemed so to me at the time, with tall locust trees, some oak and hickory, some thin maples, waist-high loosestrife, wild raspberry and other weeds, and lots of lesser undergrowth and ground cover flourishing with abandon in those forests on the sides and at the back of our house, just beyond the edged limits of the small property.

I liked to wander through those woods, not only imagining that I was exploring and relishing the idea that I was confidently on my own, but also remembering always to look over my shoulder at certain intervals to see the roof of our house so I would know I did not lose my way.

There was a stump of a long-dead cherry tree, cut about four feet up from the ground, standing defiantly in a small clearing. I often would go to it, sit down at its base, rest my back against it, twirl some leaves of grass or squish a raspberry in between my fingers, and daydream. It was a comfort to me being alone, yet knowing I was close to home.

Then one night I had a horrible nightmare.

A storm was coming up. My parents had sent me to bed early before the lightning and thunder would prevent me from falling asleep. I nestled under the thick covers to feel safe.

In my dream, I was sitting at the base of the cherry stump in the darkness. How I came to be there at night, which is something I never had done, I do not know. I was staring at the night sky, the luxuriant fabric of the stars, lost in some reverie, a dream within my dream, which I have since forgotten.

Suddenly, I was being lifted up in someone's strong hands, and in a wisp of sense and feeling I saw myself perched on the top of the stump, crouched and holding on for dear life, somehow naked, frightened, sweating, knowing, just knowing that there were many eyes watching me from in among the reeds and the trunks of the trees.

I woke and bolted up in horror and embarrassment, my heart pounding in my chest, sweating from my face and my arms and my legs, taking deep unrhythmic breaths, frightened as I never had been before.

No one was awake in the house to see me this way. It was dark in my bedroom, with vague yet eerie whispers of some strange sounds, like the ones I've always been able to hear in cemeteries, the slight gusts brushing lightly against the chiseled faces of the tombstones, now against my window pane, the leaves and the branches of the trees softly swaying in silence to the music of the wind, now sliding against the shutters, scratching them. I also heard the constant murmuring of the storm outside, as if two very different worlds were braced against each other only by our shingled roof and the aluminum siding of our house.

I soon came to realize that my dream was an omen, foretelling of later times in my life, and I now have come to understand the imagery of all of it.

The dead cherry tree, cut, a symbol for my loss of innocence. The darkness, a symbol of abandonment, loneliness, and my helplessness. My nakedness, a symbol of my constant vulnerability. The hidden, leering people, watching me at a most embarrassing and surreal moment, stripped, awkwardly struggling to keep my balance atop the trunk, the image of it all a symbol of my continuously eroding self-esteem.

Later that morning, after the storm had cleared, I set out with trepidation to go to the dead cherry stump to try to reaffirm some strength, to experience some comfort that my dream was just that, a dream, or at least to garner some satisfaction from facing it, seeing it, touching it, although all along the way I wondered if this might be a useless enterprise for me.

I kept going anyway.

When I came to the clearing, it was down, wrenched over, its root ball upended and exposed, collapsed from the massive weight of a fallen hickory tree which had crushed upon it during the storm. I stared at the haphazard network of branches, the arms of the hickory embracing the stump, and, at first, it seemed to me that the hickory's limbs were hugging the stump in a protective, almost motherly way.

And then I realized the hickory tree really was strangling it to death, again.

5

Tuesday, December 26, 2000
Manhattan

By around three o'clock in the afternoon, most of Angola's crew had drizzled into the firehouse to get ready for their shift which began promptly at 4:00 p.m. There was lively chatter and goodnaturedness, a rededication of sorts from the previous night off for the holiday, well-meaning handshakes and hugs, teasing comments and robust laughter about everyone's new jeans, new boots, scarves, jackets, gloves, jewelry, all the bounty from the day before.

Firefighter Jeremy Myers had called in sick. He was home, helping his wife comfort their infant son who was agonizingly colicky, gripped with fever, and sick with the flu. The baby's constant crying and intermittent, but uneasy napping had kept both of them up for more than seventeen hours. They had been cuddling him, watching him, cuddling him, watching him. The medicine they had received from the emergency room didn't seem to have had any effect on him. They were afraid they were losing him.

Firefighter Vanessa Fernandez was in the women's locker room. At her locker, she was holding a gold chain and gold pendant in her hand, staring at them.

The chain was thin, a box chain, but it appeared strong and durable. The pendant was heart shaped, about one inch across, with no engraving or inscription, no diamond or pearl set into it. It was simple and understated.

She placed the chain onto the hook inside her locker. The heart pendant swayed, continuing to sparkle as it lost its momentum, then came to rest.

"This will always be here for me," she whispered, "something for me to come back to. I saved you from that fire, I rescued you from the ashes." She exhaled. "That poor woman."

Lieutenant Tony Vly was on his way to the briefing room. He saw the door to the women's locker room was ajar.

He knew no one ever had bothered to attend to the bottom hinge, which was bent a little, its screws stripped. This caused the door to angle slightly from the jamb. It never shut completely. The men purposefully had left it that way for years.

He stopped for a second and peeked in. He saw Vanessa at her locker, stared at her, then brazenly entered the room to talk to her.

"Hey, Fernandez, Merry Christmas."

Vanessa still stared at the chain and pendant hanging from the hook inside her locker. "Thanks, Lieutenant," she said, as if he was inside the locker talking to her. "You, too."

Vanessa didn't mind that he was in the women's locker room.

He stood next to her. "Now that that's out of the way, you and me need to go a couple of rounds. Let's do it here and spare the rest of the shift at the briefing, okay?"

She turned to look at him.

"Now what did I do?"

Vly laced into her about her actions during the Christmas Eve fire, telling her she was in too deep, too far, separated from the others, too careless, endangering herself and her crew. He pointed his finger at her, explaining in a firm, slow voice that safety is always first, regardless of the situation.

"Rookies like you often learn their lesson after they're burned to a crisp and too dead to hear me say 'I told you so' to them, you understand me?"

She smiled demurely. "Yes, Lieutenant."

Vanessa played Tony like a pinball machine.

About three months ago, in September, a few days after Vanessa had been hired, Vly had walked by the women's locker room, peeking in unseen, as he always does. He saw Vanessa in front of her locker, alone, unbuttoning her work shirt, slowly taking it off, turning and lazily stretching to put it in her locker, and then wiggling into her turtleneck sweater, struggling a bit to get its constrictive collar over her head and its tight waist band past her breasts. He lost his composure then and breached the wall between unwitnessed voyeurism and blatant sexual harassment, boldly entering the room and telling her, "You know, Nessa, you're exotically Spanish, not like the ordinary Latinas I usually see on the streets."

Vanessa knew exactly where Tony was at that moment, not in the women's locker room, but teetering on and about to fall hard from the imagined edge of a tremendous lawsuit. And, she knew exactly where she was then, not standing before her locker, but dancing on an imagined stage in a strip joint with Tony the only leering and salivating patron in the audience.

At the time, she thought she'd keep it that way.

Vanessa was beautiful. Her hair was steely coal-black, shiny, like obsidian, long and in tight curls, a thick, stampeding expanse of numberless coiled tresses which seemed to explode off her head like errant Roman candles. Her skin was rich and silky and decadent, like dark chocolate mousse.

Whenever men saw her, they sensed volume.

She had a toned body, large, full breasts, an upper torso which gradually tapered from her wide, yet perfectly proportioned shoulders down to her thin waist, shouting a pronounced V. The men she worked for and the men she worked with thought her dainty mannerisms and her sexy, affected speech, a curious blend of hard English consonants and soft Spanish vowels, screamed a pronounced femininity and hollered a latent sensuality, even though they never considered the irony.

What was an adorable woman like that doing in a place like this?

"Yes, Lieutenant. In too far. I think I understand." She cowered a bit, nipping at the fingernail of her index finger, pulling her lips back a little, making sure Vly could see her ruby tongue flicking at it.

Staring at her mouth, he said, "Good. I'm glad we had this little conversation."

He turned away, then left the locker room.

She heard him say from the hallway, "As you were, Fernandez."

"Yes, Lieutenant," she whispered.

6

October 1955
The Old Country Road Elementary School,
Hicksville

$\mathcal{J}$n the fourth grade, I realized boys.

It was the week before Halloween, a chilly, crisp autumn day, cloudless, my classmates portioned out in huddled groups about the paved asphalt play yard, a large area screened in with chain link fence about ten feet high. Recess there always was fun for us, with our running, laughing, playing kickball, chasing each other in a game of tag, doing silly things just to stretch our legs and to feel alive after long mornings of desk work.

I remember Valerie Claremont, a friendly girl with long blonde hair and crystal green eyes, scurrying about from group to group, like a bee from flower to flower, spreading her infectious smile to all. She was the prettiest and most popular girl in our class.

That day, I saw her come before a boy who was standing alone against the fence. He seemed sullen, distracted, distant, like he was thinking of somewhere else. He was new to our class, and he looked older than the rest of us, maybe 11 or so, with his black, thick hair piled on his head in wavy clumps, his dark brown eyes like oily calamata olive pits, and he had a very slight but noticeable shadow under his nose and above his upper lip.

Valerie had run up to him, stopped, and then began talking to him. I couldn't hear her words, but I could see she seemed intent on getting something across to him in a very teasing way, curling her long, yellow-white hair with her fingers, shifting her weight from hip to hip like a really slow-ticking metronome, and arching her back. He listened to her, to every one of her words, and he seemed almost frozen with curious attention. He was smiling at her. Then, the two of them walked across the play yard, out the gate, along the side of the recess area, coming to a corner of the school building.

They disappeared around it.

After a few minutes, I walked from the yard, the same way, to where they had been. When I turned the corner of the school building, I saw the boy walking toward me, on his way back to recess, looking at me for a second as he passed me. He smiled at me.

Then I saw Valerie was sitting on the ground, leaning up against the brick wall, marionette-like, her legs bent and her arms drooping. She had a look of astonishment on her face. It was filled with amazement, as if she had just opened a birthday present in which had been a playful kitten.

I went to her.

I stood before her, looking down at her. "Hey, Val, are you okay?"

She slowly raised her head to me. She smiled that amazing smile of hers.

"I'm fine."

"Well, what happened?"

She stood up, straightened her skirt, brushed some dirt from her rear, then raised both her arms in tandem to push her hair back behind her ears with her index fingers.

She was standing there, the same way she had been with that boy at the fence, now teasing me.

"Ursula, you ever see one?" she asked me.

"One what?"

"You know, it."

"What?"

"It, a boy's thing."

Something came over me. I wanted to hear what was coming.

Valerie craned her neck forward to me, opened her eyes as large as silver dollar pancakes, then whispered to me, "Between his legs, silly."

Oh my. She started walking away from me, so I followed her.

Her words drifted over her shoulders like smoke from a chimney.

"He told me to sit down and then he stood right in front of me and then, well, you know."

"Know what?" I asked.

"He showed it to me." She giggled. "And then he told me to touch it, and I did."

Now we were walking together, about to make our last turn at the gate to get back into the recess area.

I asked her flat out, "Val, why did you do what he told you to do?"

She stopped and looked at me.

"You'll never have any boys around you, Ursula. You know why?" she asked.

"No, why?"

"Because you just don't do what they say."

She ran into the yard.

I stood there, thinking about what she had done with that boy. I was a little bothered by her actions, puzzled, but also strangely curious.

Then I understood exactly what she meant.

7

Wednesday, December 27, 2000
Hoyt Street, Brooklyn

Vanessa Fernandez was sitting on her bed. She was trying to get her get up and go to get into gear. It was 2:55 in the afternoon. Work was in sixty-five minutes, and counting.

Finally, she stood up, and then saw the wallet on the floor. She grabbed her cell phone and dialed.

A voice answered, "Yeah."

"Hey, babycakes, it's me."

She heard a condescending, pouty breath. "Now what?"

"License and registration, please."

"Damn!" the voice said. "Again?"

"Yes. It's right here on the floor. Come back and get it."

The connection faded for a moment, then cleared.

"You bring it in early for me, you understand?"

"Yes, Lieutenant."

He hung up.

She reached down and picked up Tony Vly's wallet. She held it to her breast. Then she raised it to her nose, inhaling the distinct smell of the leather. She found her backpack and slid the wallet in.

Mustn't forget it, she thought.

Earlier, Vanessa had surrendered to him.

Tony Vly was strong in so many ways. Vanessa loved to feel his chest muscles and biceps, which were as firm as apples. She loved staring into his pastel, deep-sea blue eyes, which were hypnotic to her. She yearned to feel his muscular shoulders, the ones around which she knew her arms needed to be. She just couldn't say no to him.

It had started about six weeks ago, after a shift, when they had been at Fiore's, a small, out-of-the-way tavern not far from the firehouse, a favorite spot of Tony's because of its dim lights and dark ale. They were sitting close to each other, perched on stools before the bar, just talking, doing what needed to be done to get past the superior-subordinate relationship which just didn't seem quite right or quite enough for either of them.

Tony Vly had a way with women. He knew when to thrust and when to parry, when to sting and when to caress, not only with his words, but also with his hands and his body. Vanessa loved to be in his presence, subtly exploring and then taking advantage of his moods and his desires with her sensually-voiced entendres and feigned docility. She knew exactly what she wanted from him and how to get it, and she would allow him to chase her until she caught him. And she did.

"I don't care if you are married, Tony, I just don't care," she said to him. "I just need you in my bed every now and then, don't you understand that?"

"If that's how you want it, then fine. But my rules, baby, always my rules."

She looked away from him and whispered, "Yes, Sir."

She also remembered the time in the locker room when he had watched her change her top. Of course she knew he was there eying her. She purposely had made the transition from loose soiled work shirt to tight vibrant sweater the way all men like it, slowly, with nice little detours in between so he could see her bra.

Underwear is magic, she thought.

Because of that incident and of what Tony had said to her then, Vanessa knew she could bring him down in a moment. But in her heart, she was trying to convince herself that having him this way, on his beck and call basis, was an opportunity for her to feel at least some control over him in particular, and, in an odd way, over all men in general. Obviously, if he becked, then it was up to her to call, right?

That was control, wasn't it?

Control. She understood it was something she inevitably was damned to experience from men. Yet, deep down inside, she knew she wasn't kidding herself to think she actually exerted it over them.

Nevertheless, she realized that nearly everything with Tony, and with all her men, was part and parcel of a powerless yet intriguing and addicting situation for her, one of rampant desire and unbridled lust, but for some reason, it was one which she had craved.

8

November 1958
Monroe Street, Hicksville

$\mathcal{W}$hen I was in the seventh grade, my parents allowed me to go to my first party.

My friend Francine's birthday was the 11th, which I think was a Tuesday and a school night, so her party was the following Friday.

Francine's school locker was near mine, so we sometimes found ourselves walking the halls together, and she was in a few of my classes, so we sometimes did group work together.

Francine was a year older than I was, tall for her age, like me, and skinny and dark. Her skin looked like caramel even though both her parents were as white as marshmallows, just like mine. Her black hair was long and curly, her fingers thin like pencils, and her body, for a thirteen-year-old who now was officially a teenager, was perfect. She had long, shapely legs, broad shoulders, a skinny waist, and tulipy breasts which seemed very proud to be where they were on her.

She lived about three blocks from me. We gradually had become close friends. We often found each other outside after school was over, and we would walk home together through the neighborhood, talking about boys, school, movies, teachers, records, makeup, clothes, parents, dolls, boys, and whatever else had held our interests at the time.

In school that Friday, the talk among our small group of budding young-stuff heartbreakers—what Francine's older brother had called us, Francine, Lynn, Gloria, and me—was all about her party.

Francine's brother was 19, almost 20, and she told us that she had asked him, that she had begged him, to get some of his friends to come. We were so excited that there might be some real live older boys to mingle with because, well, most of the boys our age were just wormballs. To us, they seemed so immature and too playful, overbearingly silly, and most often more interested in themselves and in each other rather than in us. Baseball and airplanes, cars and television, seemed the only things they really ever focused on for long.

That night, my father drove me to the party.

I remember hearing the rain plopping on the windshield and my father's voice in a sort of counterpoint of monotones, although I really wasn't listening to what he was saying. I was listening to the drops.

Stepping into Francine's house, I remember chirping a hello to her parents, handing my gift to her, an Elvis Presley album wrapped in silver paper with a red bow, then following her down the stairs to the basement.

Music was playing. It was "Maybe" by the Chantels.

Earlier that day, Francine's parents had arranged some folding chairs along two of the basement walls and had opened a bridge table against the third to hold napkins, cups, chips, popcorn and punch, and a small phonograph and piles of records. I saw a rickety wooden stand in the corner with a gooseneck desk lamp on it which made a warm glow.

Boys were everywhere.

At the bottom of the stairs, Francine turned around to me and hugged me. I smelled her perfume. It was sweet. I didn't have any on.

"Isn't this great, Urse?" She could barely contain her excitement.

"Yes, yes, it's great, Fran!" I said.

Now I heard Elvis Presley singing "Anyway You Want Me." Then, I looked over her shoulder and saw a god.

"Fran, Fran, who's that boy over there in the black vest?"

She turned around for a second, then back to me. She hunched her shoulders and raised her hand to her mouth to hide her wide smile. Then she came closer to me, whispering in my ear, "That's Bobby Titus."

The first thing I thought was, Mrs. Ursula Titus.

"He works with my brother at the Esso station. Isn't he adorable?"

Words cannot express what I felt at that moment.

Sometime later, someone had unscrewed the bulb in the desk lamp. The basement was then nearly dark, only a slight glow from the well of stairs and the lighted kitchen above, a ray faint and low.

Out of nowhere, Bobby Titus came up to me, clamping his strong hands around my elbows, pushing me backward toward the small area where couples were slow-dancing. He looked down at me, smiling. I took several steps in retreat until he stopped me. Then, he took my hands and placed them behind his neck. I clasped my fingers and held them there. He reached behind me and pressed his palms against the small of my back. I felt my small chest press into his. He embraced me, hugging me tightly, opening his legs so mine could fit in between his as we danced.

And then I felt something else.

Valerie Claremont must have closed the door at the top of the cellar stairs on her way back down to the basement from the bathroom upstairs. Now it was nearly pitch black. I kept dancing in Bobby Titus' arms, understanding from his body language that he wanted me to press into him harder and slowly sway my hips from side to side so there was friction between us, my chest to his, my stomach to his, my, well, you know, to his, too.

After our dance, he took me by the hand. With me in tow, he pushed through some kids who were still locked in swooning embraces, kissing, still slow-dancing, although the music temporarily had stopped. From the corner of my eye, I saw Marlene

Wagner sifting through the piles of 45's, apparently looking for a special song.

Bobby Titus led me behind the cellar stairs, which were parallel to and about six feet out from the fourth wall of the basement. In between the stairs and the wall, a couch had been tucked away to remove it from the center of the basement space to give us a place to dance.

Appropriately, it was a love seat.

I heard the Chantels again, "Maybe."

My girlfriend Lynn Rankle was on the couch, lazily slouched back with her butt about to fall off the edge of the cushion, both her hands nested behind her head, her legs wide apart, her body pressed down by the weight of Andy Wassmer, who was on her lap straddling her. He was all over her. Her blouse was open, her bra undone and pushed up to her neck. They were kissing as Andy explored her chest with his hands.

Still holding my hand, Bobby Titus sat down in the small space next to Lynn and Andy. He pulled me toward him. I had to straddle his lap, too, to sit on him facing him, my hands on his shoulders, because with Lynn and Andy working out with each other, there wasn't enough room for me to get next to him.

Grabbing my hair, he pulled my face closer to his, and then he kissed me.

Hard.

And good.

Soon I was reeling, sitting on his bulge, feeling his hands all over me, his wet kisses at the base of my neck and along my collar bones, his fingers tugging at the last two buttons of my blouse.

Then it seemed another set of his hands was squeezing my butt. Then he slid one hand under my skirt and up my thighs, the knuckles of his fist beginning to brush up and down against the front of my cotton panties, right where I suddenly wanted them to be. His other hand opened my bra in an instant. He was kissing my breasts.

I heard the Chantels again.

That same song, over and over.

He kissed me more, then put his hands on my shoulders and pushed me down.

I surrendered.

I slid off him and was on my knees on the floor before him, snug between his open legs.

He quickly unzippered his pants.

There it was.

Then I was tasting him, feeling his hands cupped behind my head, slowly guiding me up and down.

Then a spasm, then another, and then another.

I gagged.

He moaned, as loudly as a locomotive in a tunnel.

Later, I remember opening the passenger-side door of my father's car. He was smiling at me as I got in. "How was the party, Ursula?"

"It was great, Dad, great. Thanks for letting me go."

He smiled. "You're a young lady now, my dear, and you need to experience the company of other young adults in a social setting."

I smiled back at him. "Right, Dad."

The ride home seemed long. Raindrops were plopping on the windshield again and the drone of the wipers made my mind wander. But not too far. I was thinking about what I had done, how fast all of it had happened, and yet how slow it all had been for me, like the music, that Chantels' song, the hypnotic "Maybe," and then "I'm So Young," then "Lovers Never Say Goodbye" and "A Thousand Miles Away," some tunes by Johnny Mathis, then the Chantels again, over and over and over.

Everything had just fallen into place. I had fallen.

When we got home, my mother ushered us into the house. She was curious to know everything from me and from my father, hoping that I would tell her everything first and then she would hear it again from him, whatever she thought I already had told him in the car.

I told both of them next to nothing.

After brushing my teeth three separate times, I went to bed. I lay there, staring at the ceiling. I soon fell asleep.

Early Saturday morning, the telephone rang. It was Francine. She told me that she had done what I did, Lynn had done what I did, and Gloria had done what I did.

We all had done it.

There were four boys somewhere, probably sleeping soundly in their beds right then, gloating in their dreams that they had had their way with us.

After she hung up, I went to the bathroom to brush my teeth again.

Hard.

And long.

I was staring into the mirror, wondering what Bobby Titus' voice must sound like.

He hadn't said one word to me the entire time.

9

Thursday, December 28, 2000
Manhattan

Captain Tom Angola and Lieutenant Tony Vly were nearly drunk.

They had come to Fiore's after their shift, now loitering on stools with pints of dark ale and piles of salty peanuts in front of them on the bar. Neither man wanted to go home.

After an hour or so of small talk, Angola said, "I just can't keep my eyes off her, Tone."

Vly lit another cigarette, not realizing there was one smoking in the ashtray.

"I know, Tom, there's something about that broad. She's such a looker. Such magnetism."

Tom sipped some ale. "And that accent she's got, so slight, but it still colors her words. It's freakin' music."

"For sure. You notice her boobs always bounce a little when she talks? I do. I could watch and listen to her go on all night about anything, the weather, pot roast recipes, directions to Jersey, whatever."

Angola looked ahead, into the mirror behind the glass shelves stocked with liquor bottles, raking his fingers through his hair. "Man, I'd do her in a minute."

Tony now looked ahead, his eyes meeting Tom's in the mirror. Tony couldn't contain the smile which had just erupted like a volcano, full-blown on his face.

"You bastard!" Tom shouted, slapping Tony's forearm hard with the palm of his hand.

"Hey, what can I tell you, Captain."

"You son of a bitch!" Tom said.

Tony Vly was thinking about the passion of using and abusing Vanessa yesterday, and the many times before that, the way she liked it rough, her playful struggling which only made him hotter, his tossing of her around on the bed, slapping her ass, pulling her hair, taking her from behind and watching her softball-sized melons hanging down and then bouncing back and forth in a steady rhythm as he pounded her hard and fast.

Tom Angola was fantasizing about Tony doing her, as if he was standing there watching them. Tom imagined Vanessa on her back, her legs open, his good friend Tony pressing down into her, screwing her like a piston, seeing her legs coming up around Tony's torso, her ankles locking, her holding onto him for dear life.

"How long?" Tom asked.

Tony dragged again on another cigarette. "Not long enough, pal."

They laughed.

After a few moments of silence, Tom said, "I'd pay money for a shot at her."

Tony slowly sipped his ale.

Then he said, "Maybe I can get you a freebie."

10

*November 1961
The Manor Apartments, Westbury*

$\mathcal{I}$ was fifteen when my body was on fire for the first time.

I felt a stinging pain deep inside me, searing from between my legs to my thighs, down my legs to my calves, and then to my toes. The slimy wetness of my skin and the choking smell of smoke prodded me to get up, get up, to run, run, to distance myself from the heat I was feeling. I struggled, twisting and turning, but the boy's moving weight kept me down. The sweet agony of that burning, that strange feeling of passion and excitement on the thin white-hot line between pain and pleasure, was rising within me.

It was my first time.

Then a sudden smothering across my mouth increased my panic. The boy was kissing me relentlessly. I couldn't catch my breath.

Again I struggled with him, but finally managed to respond to him with kisses and licks. I was cringing from the fiery pressure between my legs, the weight of him on me and off me, on me and off me, on me and off me, and then I felt release.

I opened my eyes.

My sweet blessed nightmare was over. It had come while I lay in this bed. I felt my perspiration, beads of sweat like little diamonds on my stomach, on my thighs, at the small of my back and under my arms.

I smelled.

It had happened.

The boy was still on top of me, dozing. The sheets were damp. His cigarette smoldered in the tabled ashtray next to the bed, igniting other butts, the smoke lingering about us. The boy was breathing deeply.

Slowly, I rolled him off me, then got up from the bed. I felt an ache in my jaw. It hurt, bad. My lips were swollen, too. Was it from so much kissing, or from the strain earlier in the evening when he and I were walking from the mall, hunched over, trudging through the bitter cold through the deserted streets of the neighborhood to his apartment, my mouth clamped shut to prevent my teeth from snapping like mouse traps?

We had stopped along the way when we saw the accident scene. It looked like an ambulance had been hit broadside in an intersection by a white Plymouth coupe, its negligent driver apparently oblivious to the siren. I remember staring at the policeman there, tasting the cold in the air, listening to the orchestra of sounds, always the sounds, the wind, the muffled, static voice from the police car radio, the drivers yelling at each other, the hums from a slowly moving line of other cars crawling past the scene. I even could hear the drivers' heads turning when they craned their necks to see what had happened as they idled by.

Now my thighs hurt. I looked at them to see bruises had surfaced, blue-red bursts of swelling. I don't remember how I got them. In my hair, I smelled the beginning of winter from the air outside and the acrid smoke from inside this room. My fingers were cold.

It had been a long night for me.

It had started when Francine and I went to the mall around dinner time to shop. We met two boys there. They were older, telling us they were in college. They followed us around from store to store, constantly talking to us, frequently making us laugh. They bought us salty soft pretzels and sodas.

When we got to Gertz, the department store anchor at the mall, I remember Francine thinking up a silly game as we strolled through the girls' clothing section. She told the boys to pick out things they wanted to see us try on. "We'll put the stuff on and then like model for you, okay?"

They both said, "Sure."

Francine looked at me, waiting.

I said, "Um, okay."

They walked off to find some things for us. Francine and I just stood there, waiting for them to come back to us.

They quickly returned, opting for a skirt and a cardigan sweater for me, and just a full-length slip for her. They wanted to see Francine's body, up close and personal.

When they handed the clothes to us, we went toward the bank of stalls to try them on.

One of the boys said, "Get in that one together."

Francine and I turned to look at each other.

Something came over us.

We went into the same stall.

The taller boy slowly swung the door toward its latch to close it, but he kept it open just a bit. The other boy was on tiptoes peeking over his shoulder at us.

The taller boy said, "Well, go ahead."

Francine put the slip down on the bench right there and then started to take off her dungarees. Leaning over to get one pants leg past her shoe, she looked at me, with strands of her hair lazily draped across he face. "Do it, Urse, it'll be fun."

I put the sweater and the skirt on the bench. I sat down and started to take off my sneakers. Then I looked up at Francine and saw she was standing there in her underwear, just in her panties and her bra. The boys were looking at her, smirking. I thought I heard the shorter boy beginning to salivate.

Soon, I, too, was done undressing, sitting there just in my underwear.

"Nice, nice," one of the boys said, "now put them on."

Francine took off her bra, then her panties.

It was the first time in my life I was in the presence of a totally undressed girl. I could tell it wasn't the first time for the boys.

Francine slowly put on the slip. She raised both her arms high in the air and wiggled. Then she rested her hands on the top of her head, lacing her fingers together, smiling at the boys. I stood up, put on the skirt, then the sweater, but I didn't button it.

They stared at us. We rotated for them.

Then the taller boy said, "Nice. Okay, good girls. Now take them off and put your clothes back on and let's get out of here."

They watched us change back. Then we left the store.

Francine and I made our calls.

I told my parents I was sleeping over at Francine's and she told her parents she was sleeping at my house. We had to fix things so she could be with the taller boy, Randy, I think that was his name, at his place, and I could be with this boy here in this apartment.

It all had happened so fast, and here I am.

I tiptoed to the bathroom.

The water hissed and spurted, then pulsed, then settled to a nice steady drone. The shower felt good.

I heard the water whisper to me. Virgin.

I pressed my chest against the tiled wall as the hot spray pelted my back. My butt cheeks ached, they were really sore.

Then I heard the water whisper again. Vixen.

The streams embraced me, whatever I was.

I suddenly realized I had been transformed, forever.

I stood motionless there in the shower-rain, wondering.

What was this guy's name again?

11

Friday, December 29, 2000
Risoli's Roman Gardens, Forest Hills

The annual holiday party for the station house always has been held during the stretch of days between Christmas Day and New Year's Eve. The crew was given the night off, permitted to use their accumulated compensatory time, as long as coverage for their shift could be guaranteed. The Captains from several of the firehouses on the East Side worked in concert to make sure this would happen, lending their men and women in checkerboard fashion, so all the units could celebrate the holidays with their own parties.

Each year, Captain Tom Angola gave the opportunity, no, the assignment, to someone in the unit to book a cozy place offering accommodations for sixty firefighters and staff and their partners, a small but varied buffet, an open bar, and room for dancing.

Because she was the rookie, three days junior to Jeremy Myers, Vanessa's turn came now.

She booked Risoli's in Forest Hills because her grandfather knew Risoli from the service. During World War II, they were with the 53rd Weather Reconnaissance Squadron together, serving their tours of duty with honor, although not with much distinction in the Pacific Theater. Nothing too exciting really ever happened with the weather, except for maybe a renegade tornado every once in a while swirling through the Philippines, or a random hurricane every now and then marauding its way across Borneo. After their military obligations were over, Vanessa's grandfather went into the restaurant supply business so he could visit his customers and eat for free, and Risoli had bought what used to be the old Hodge Funeral Home, turning it into a modest catering service and party business, so he always could be where the action was.

Since this was her first try at planning a party, Vanessa made sure she took care of everything.

During the past few weeks, she had asked many of her coworkers about previous holiday parties, about what worked and what hadn't. She quickly learned that what they wanted was simple: food, drink, and dancing. And plenty of it.

The food. She contracted for garden salad, roast beef, baked ham, sausage and peppers, shrimp lo mein, baked ziti, broiled scallops, barbecued ribs and chicken, steamed egg noodles, fresh string beans and cauliflower, and her favorite, arroz con pollo.

That should cover the ethnic and dietary spreads, she had thought.

The drinks. Knowing that underestimating and having the well run dry half way through the night just wouldn't cut it with this bunch, she ordered plenty of the liquid stuff: bourbon, scotch, rye, gin, vodka, rum, Pinot Grigio, French Colombard, Chardonnay, Burgundy, blush Chablis, Miller, Foster's, Corona, Heiniken, and peppermint schnapps. Just to be on the safe side, she added Pepsi and diet Pepsi, and pitchers of ice water with lemon.

She even remembered sliced fruit and assorted nuts.

Everybody had said they loved sweets, so she ordered an assortment of butter cookies and a double-chocolate sheet cake with strawberries, and vanilla ice cream.

She also had called Fiore's and asked what kinds of ale were served there. She ordered two kinds.

Now I need music, she had thought.

One of Vanessa's girlfriends, Brenda Villanueva, whom she had known since elementary school, lived in Vanessa's building, upstairs in the third floor apartment. After graduating from high school, they had gone apartment hunting together, planning on sharing one, but when they saw the two vacant apartments on Hoyt Street, newly renovated and freshly painted, they immediately decided to take them both. They had wanted to live together, but this was even better for them.

Brenda was seeing a Spanish guy from Flatbush. He had tons of sound equipment and thousands of albums, so Vanessa arranged for him to be the deejay. "Lots of upbeat stuff, pop, rock, country and western, R and B, some heavy metal, salsa, lots of oldies, even disco," she had told him, "but no rap!" She had drawn the line there.

The party was wonderful. Nearly all the squad had come. The food was good, the drinks strong, cold and wet, the music loud, and the dancing divine.

It was fun for Vanessa to see her coworkers enjoying themselves without the demons of fear, tension and anxiety in their eyes. She could sense their relaxation, guarded as it was, as they ate and drank and danced, as if the pressures from their jobs temporarily had been released from rusty valves somewhere deep inside them.

Then, there was an awkward moment.

It was like the times when everything among gathered friends is proceeding very orderly and expectedly, the give and take of banter, the warm congeniality, the good humor which is amusing to all, and then, all of a sudden, something is said by someone which changes the atmosphere for everyone, realigning the very atoms in the air they are breathing, a few passing, seemingly innocent words which mutate the pleasing and casual moments of conversation and companionship into an insufferable eternity of discomfort, jealousy and anger.

Vanessa and Jeremy Myers were standing with their backs to the bar watching everyone.

Jeremy's wife was home with their infant son who still was ill, but slowly recovering. Vanessa had come alone, too, so Jeremy had suggested it would be a good idea for them to hang out together, sit at the same table, and maybe dance a little with each other. This way, he reasoned, as rookies, they both would feel tethered to the rest of the group socially, not just professionally. She had said okay.

Vanessa was licking the rim of her wine glass when Lieutenant Tony Vly walked up, stood beside her at the bar, snapped his fingers for the bartender, and ordered an ale.

Without looking at her, he said out of the side of his mouth, low enough so Jeremy, on the other side of her, couldn't hear. "Killer dress, Nessa."

"Thank you, Sir." She emphasized her reply with staccato breaths in between her words.

She kept licking the rim of her wine glass, knowing Tony could see her doing it with his peripheral vision. Jeremy was looking around, anticipating an awkward moment coming.

Not yet.

For several days now, Jeremy sensed there was electricity between Vanessa and Tony, but he kept his suspicions to himself, instead fantasizing about her the way he always did, how she must look naked, and how she would perform in bed. He lusted for her, too.

Vanessa was looking at the dance floor, watching a few couples trying to get the hang of line dancing. Tony was leaning into the bar, his elbows on the counter, sipping the ale. "It fits you like a fucking glove," he moaned.

Pinball time again.

She spoke softly into her wine glass. "Well, it's a chemise, Lieutenant. It's supposed to be worn as a slip, not really as a dress."

"Yeah, I know," he said.

Vanessa's chemise was black. And tight. And short. Its two thin spaghetti straps strained from the monumental task of keeping her full breasts contained within its bodice. Its side seams were stressed with tension, but holding. It had a slit on the left side, cut up enough to reveal the lacy top of her stocking.

"Garters, right Nessa?" Tony asked, looking into his glass.

"Yes, Sir." More breaths.

Underwear is magic, she thought.

Tony put his drink down. Using matches from the bar, he lit a cigarette. After he shook the flame out, he threw the match toward the ashtray. It bounced on the rim and landed on the bar.

"Looks like you missed the hole, Sir."

He looked down at the floor trying to conceal his smile. He saw her shoes. Black, open-toed stilettos with thin ankle straps and three-inch heels. No, four.

For now, that was enough for him.

As he started to turn to go back to his table, a woman passing by bumped into him, almost dropping the glass which seemed to be pulling her right hand and dragging her toward Tony. She was a little tipsy.

Now, "Stayin' Alive" by the BeeGees played.

"Wellloookkkwho'ssshereee!" the woman giggled to him.

She stretched up to kiss him on the lips.

He kissed back on her mouth. "Mmmmmmm," he said, "still sweet."

"Hi, I'm Vanessa. This is Jeremy."

Testing her legs for balance, the woman quickly looked at Jeremy, then slowly stared Vanessa up and down.

"Hi there, I'm Gail, Tony's wife."

Gail laced her left arm under Tony's sports jacket and around his waist, smiling as if to say 'He's mine,' but she really needed something to hold on to in order to steady herself.

Vanessa said, "Hi, Gail. We've all heard so much about you. Wow, you're much prettier than Tony said you were."

There was a brood of female alley cats hissing in chorus somewhere, or so it seemed.

There was silence.

Jeremy turned to look away. He was thinking, Here's another broad who needs to be taught a lesson when to keep her mouth shut, and when to keep it open.

Then, hesitant laughter.

"Hey, wait a second there guys," Tony said, "I've always

been one for understatement, you know that, Gail, right?"

Gail forced a smile, then sipped her drink unsteadily.

"Yes, darling," she blurted, "with everything except your magnificent plumbing."

They all laughed.

Then Vanessa said, "Well, Tony's never been short on length, girth or width."

There was silence, again.

The uninvited guest, the quintessential awkward moment, had arrived.

"Realllllly," Gail said defensively.

"No, no," Jeremy leaned in, "come on now, she means with the fire hoses. Tony can always tell the gauge. Some talent, wouldn't you say?"

Gail pondered that for a moment. Her eyes turned cold.

Oldies time. The Chantels now, "Maybe."

"I think I need to dance, Tony."

She plodded away toward the dance floor.

Jeremy excused himself, going to the men's room.

Tony barked at Vanessa through tight lips. "You bitch. You know I'm going to beat you for that next time."

Vanessa licked the rim of her wine glass again.

"I know, Lieutenant, and I deserve it. But I can't wait 'til tomorrow so instead Jeremy's going to do it to me later tonight, okay?"

The pinball machine again.

Tilt.

Broiling, Tony went off to dance with his wife.

12

*June 25, 1964 — Graduation Day
Hicksville High School*

$\mathcal{I}$ really don't remember much of my preparation for my high school graduation day, eating breakfast, getting dressed, even going to the school or actually being there, except for two incidents which are still branded in my memory. And when I think about them, they're rather like faded photographs which somehow vibrantly come to life, like movies.

One was when the ceremony was about to begin. I was walking down an aisle in the auditorium in between Curtis Ralls and Danny Ruiz, two boys I had known from another one of Francine LaMonica's parties.

That was February last, around Valentine's Day, and what made that party so special was Francine's parents had gone to Atlantic City for the weekend to attend an awards presentation for Mr. LaMonica to celebrate his twenty-five years of service to some fraternal organization which he belonged to, and then for them to have a little fun at the casinos.

For us, that meant no nosy chaperones.

Francine's brother, Michael, was 25 years old then, so her parents had left him in charge, but all he did that weekend was to spend almost the entire time with their cousin Richard, who was 27. Richard lived in a studio apartment somewhere in Hempstead. They went to a car show at Roosevelt Field Mall on

Friday night, slept in at Richard's, and then Saturday morning took the train into New York City, spending all day there. They came back to Richard's late Saturday night, slept in, then returned to the city for most of Sunday. Francine later told me that during those two days, Michael and Richard had gone to as many all-day and all-night peep shows and seedy topless bars and strip joints as they could fit into the nearly nineteen hours they were in Manhattan. Then, Michael came home to Monroe Street late Sunday afternoon, around 4:00 p.m., just under the wire. Good thing. The LaMonica's noisy blue Buick had coughed into the driveway at 4:25.

Because my high school was so overcrowded, on double shifts to accommodate the massive throngs of kids from our town, I didn't really know Danny Ruiz and Curtis Ralls until Francine's party. Prior to that, I was aware of them just by sight and by name. I often had seen them in the halls, and Lynn had dated Danny and Gloria had dated Curtis, so the word about them had gotten around to me. They were fun.

In the auditorium, we all sat down together, Curtis on my right and Danny on my left. They looked like animated bookends, each turning his head toward me to talk to me.

Danny told me to meet them later at the Green.

The Green they meant was the small strip mall, not too far from the school, up off a side street from Division Avenue, just over the borderline between Hicksville and Levittown. Several Greens, little outposts of commerce complete with small shops, delis, dry cleaners, candy stores and even swimming pools and picnic areas, were peppered throughout the enormous Levittown housing complex. I had been to them all.

I said to Danny, "Maybe. Maybe I will."

Hearing the hesitancy in my voice, Curtis then leaned into my ear and whispered to me that they really needed me to be there for them. "It's lesson time for you again," he said.

I knew exactly what he meant.

I didn't say anything to him just then because I was thinking about Francine's Valentine's Day heartbreaker party.

Her house was dark inside. There was music. There was beer. There were boys.

I remember standing in the kitchen, flirting with Curtis, while Francine was pairing off with a boy named Vincent, going into the den with him. Lynn was dancing in the living room with a tall, nice-looking Italian guy. Gloria was on her way up the stairs with Roger in tow to Francine's parents' king-sized bed. I was left in the kitchen with Curtis.

Then, the doorbell rang.

I walked with Curtis to answer it. Just before he opened the door, he lurched at me, kissing me.

At the door, there was Danny Ruiz, alone. He came inside. Without saying anything to me, he kissed me hello.

In the calm of that moment, I could hear the both of them breathing slowly.

Something just came over me.

Somehow I later found myself with Curtis and Danny inside the large walk-in closet in Francine's parents' bedroom. Curtis and Danny were kissing me, fondling me, teasing me, squeezing me, playfully pulling at my clothes. It was exciting to experience two boys paying so much attention to me at the same time. A threesome was new to me.

Then I heard muffled rustling from the bed, like its sheets were being angrily stripped from it, the pillowcases forcefully being pulled from the pillows. But I knew those sounds were from under the covers, Gloria's satin top, corduroy slacks, and underwear coming off, fast. Really fast.

Suddenly, I was scared for her, and for me. I knew what Roger wanted from her, and I knew what Curtis and Danny wanted from me.

I had done it for the first time a few years ago, and ever since then, in the back of my mind, I kept thinking about myself as the defenseless, dead cherry tree from my nightmare, and how I had been strangled to death that night by the arms and by the hands of that boy who had kissed me, stripped me, slapped me across my face for speaking to him when I hadn't been spoken to, how he had punched my thighs to make me open my legs wider, spanked my butt for being contrary to him when I didn't want him on top of me, and then forced himself on me in his small apartment in Westbury. I've always felt that night with him wasn't a beginning for me, but rather an end, not a birth, but a death, my virginity a spirit no longer alive in me, my innocence dearly departed, something no longer a part of me, something regrettably lost, forever irretrievable.

Parting really is such sweet sorrow.

I hadn't done it since then, and I didn't want Curtis and Danny to do it to me now.

They were relentless with me, like an army of ants swarming over a spilled cup of orange soda. I tried to defend myself from their advances, but I couldn't. They were too strong. I was weeping, pushing them away, telling them I would scream if they did it to me.

Danny stepped around behind me and held my arms to my back. Struggling, I tried to turn, I tried to free myself. I was kicking Danny, and Curtis, too, who was busy in front of me fidgeting with my blouse buttons and my dungaree zipper. I kept telling them I would scream, I'll scream, I'll scream. Curtis kept telling me I wouldn't, No you won't, No you won't.

Then I was naked, feeling Curtis' hands sliding all over my body. He was out of control, kissing me, licking me, squeezing my breasts, nipping with his teeth at my neck, feeling my ass, pulling his fist up between my legs, almost lifting me off the floor.

I didn't know what else to do, so I spit at him.

He was enraged, slapping me hard across my face.

I stopped struggling.

My jaw hurt.

Curtis grabbed me by my hair and pulled down hard, forcing me to my knees. Danny still held my arms behind my back. Curtis looked down at me, seeing I was petrified. Somehow, he seemed to come to his senses, telling me he wasn't going to rape me, but he would make damned sure I understood my place with him. He opened his chinos. He pulled my hair toward him so my face was buried between his legs. I started doing what he wanted me to do.

I remember hearing Gloria from the bed, her short breaths and huffy moans bursting in between the sound of a steady tempo, the mattress inhaling and exhaling from the weight of Roger ceaselessly thrusting into her and backing out of her. She kept moaning and moaning.

Then, I felt a spasm, then another, and then another.

I was gagging, trying to swallow and to breathe at the same time. Curtis slapped me hard across my face again, then slipped behind me to hold my arms. Now Danny was in front of me. It was his turn to teach me my lesson. He did.

I heard a loud screech and then muffled thumps from the microphone as the principal, old Mrs. Rayzak, stood poised tapping on it with her fingernail from behind a weathered wooden lectern, then starting the graduation ceremony by introducing herself and the members of the Board of Education who were seated on metal chairs behind her.

I tuned out, turning to look at Curtis, who was still waiting for my reply.

I said, "Maybe." Then I smiled at him and kissed him quickly on the lips. I saw the excitement and the frustration in his eyes.

The other frame of memory I have of that day was after the ceremony was over. I was walking across the football field, trying to locate my parents among what seemed to me to be countless desert sands of kids, teachers, parents, relatives and siblings.

Along the way, I saw Mr. Henry standing alone by one of the goal posts. I started walking toward him.

Because of some scheduling flukes, Mr. Henry had been my English teacher for three years in a row, for grades 10, 11 and 12. All my friends believed that must have been an absolute torture for me, and for him, too. But in my mind, I relished every one of his classes, every single one, and his constant enthusiasm for literature and for writing, his wonderful, moving and expressive way of reading aloud to us in class, his love of Greek mythology, which was his favorite unit, mine, too, and his varied choices of reading selections and assignments.

I remember one in particular. For our senior project, he told us to pick an author who was dead and to read everything the author had ever written. Our reports were to be thorough and comprehensive, interesting and well-written, perceptive and pervasive. He was curious, he had said, to read our comments about and our reactions to an author's entire body of work. He insisted our comparisons and contrasts touch on style, theme, tone, mood, historical background, character analysis and character interaction. Everyone else in our class choked at the thought of this endeavor, but I couldn't wait to get started. For some reason, I chose Honoré de Balzac, starting with *Pere Goriot* and *A Harlot's Progress*.

I also remember that during those three years, no one ever had misbehaved in Mr. Henry's classes. There wasn't time to. There were too many fun things to do, all the interesting activities hiding the learning and the work. Everyone just loved his daily excitement for words, vocabulary, thoughts and ideas, and the nuances of our language. Everyday, he started his class standing at the front of the room, usually holding a visual aid in his hands or with something scribbled on the chalkboard, highlighting what we would be doing. From the bell's last echo to signal the beginning of class, until its sounding forty-five minutes later, all of us were mesmerized.

Every day, I desperately needed to hear from him what came to be his never ending encouragement and kind supportive words to me to write, write, write. He had said I had a provocative way with words. Surely he would know. In all, he must have read more than three hundred of my essays, compositions, thought pieces, poems, reports, stories, paragraph responses and research papers.

Mr. David Henry was almost three inches shorter than I was, rake thin, his bushy salt and pepper hair always so wiry and untamed, like hordes of alien weeds trying to free themselves from his head. His luminous brown eyes were almost hidden behind the funny glasses he always wore, their thick bottle lenses and wide black frame making him look moronic in a way.

But none of that mattered to me.

To me, he was handsome, and adorably so.

In my heart, I knew I loved him then.

I often daydreamed I was his wife and he was my husband, and everyday in class we only pretended that he was just my teacher and that I was just his student. I fantasized that after school we would leave from separate exits, then meet each other under the cover of darkness at our cozy little house, kiss and hug, and then I would always give him what he wanted.

Me.

Of course, we kept our secret safe from all those who just wouldn't understand how a seventeen-year-old girl could totally surrender herself to a man old enough to be her father.

Mr. Henry was forty-eight.

I walked up to him in the end zone and said hello.

He smiled his warm smile to me, told me how proud he was of me and my work, and then wished me the best for what he was sure lay ahead of me, a long and successful career as a writer.

I put my hand on his shoulder, leaned down to him, and kissed him on the cheek. He blushed.

My heart melted at that moment.

Then I told him my parents had given me permission to go to the Green in a little while to meet some friends and that I could stay out until midnight. This was a lie, of course, since I hadn't even met up with them yet, but I said it anyway. I knew if I had to, I could get them to let me disappear until the witching hour.

He looked at me in a puzzled way, like when he would wrestle with us in class with subject-verb agreement or sentence diagramming.

I know he sensed the entendre in my voice.

An awkward moment went by.

I felt like we were standing together, face to face, holding hands on a paper-thin sheet of ice floating on the Atlantic, thousands of miles from any shoreline, just waiting for the ice to give way so I could drown with him in my arms.

I took a deep breath.

Then, the words just flew out of my mouth.

I begged him, I pleaded with him, "Meet me, take me somewhere, anywhere, be with me, please Mr. Henry, please, please, I love you, I'll do whatever you tell me to do, I swear it."

He was startled, taking a step back from me, his eyes exploding open with astonishment from behind his glasses. I frantically went toward him with my arms outstretched, trying to embrace him, trying to kiss him again, this time on the lips. He fought me off.

Then he told me it could not be.

I was devastated.

I wanted never to see him again.

13

Saturday, December 30, 2000
Forest Hills

In the middle of the empty banquet room at Risoli's, Vanessa Fernandez was looking at her watch. It was 1:35 a.m. She was alone. The party had been a huge success. She had just finished settling up with Mr. Risoli, handing him a wad of cash collected from her coworkers, and everything came out to the penny. Vanessa had kissed him on the forehead and he had pinched her cheek, lovingly, telling her to give his warm regards to her grandfather. She said she would.

Vanessa went toward the coat room and saw Jeremy Myers with his back to her, reaching to get his woolen coat from a hangar.

At six-two, Jeremy was as tall as a lighthouse, and powerfully built. His skin was tightly pulled over his muscles. His light brown hair was streaked with blond. His face was almost square, rugged, with high cheekbones and a jaw like iron. But his lips were soft, like two slender beds of roses planted in the middle of a concrete runway. His hazel eyes sparkled.

"Hey, Jeremy, you still here?"

He turned to Vanessa's voice.

"Nessa! Yep, on my way home right now."

She noticed his eyes slowly dropping, staring for three seconds at her neck, then for three more at her breasts, three at her waist, three at the little slit in her chemise, three at her legs and another three at her high heels.

Then he quickly looked back up into her eyes.

She smiled at him. In one fluid motion she opened her legs a little, shifting her weight onto her left leg, pointed her toes inwardly, then placed her left hand on her hip.

"How's the movie, Jeremy?"

He pushed out his breath. "Riveting, Van, four stars."

She kissed him on the cheek.

"Well," he said, turning back around to the coat rack, "this one must be yours, it's the only one left." He took her black leather, waist-length bolero jacket from its place.

"Here, let me hold it for you." He presented it to her.

She turned around and slid her arms into the sleeves.

"And why don't you let me hold it for you, Jeremy?" she asked coyly.

They both laughed.

She turned back around, facing him.

"Let's go, okay?" she asked.

They walked together from the room, down the stairs, then out back into the parking lot. The air was crisp and clean, chilling, yet invigorating.

They went to Vanessa's car.

"I've always loved your wheels, Van."

"Thanks, Jeremy. I love it, too. It's a '78. My dad gave it to me when his midlife crisis stopped after my mom told him it was either her or this car, so now it's mine. Guys just love seeing a girl drive a 'Vette."

"Yes, they sure do," he said. He pointed to his vehicle three spaces over. His tone changed. "And here I am, scooting around town in a minivan. Women hate minivans, don't they?"

She smiled. "Of course not, silly." Then she took a step closer to him and reached with her index finger to touch his chin.

Suddenly, he grabbed onto her lapels, pulling her into him, kissing her passionately on the lips, flicking his tongue, licking her lips in between the words saying, "You love my minivan, don't you, Nessa," kissing her again and again.

He felt her struggle momentarily, then succumb to him, her breasts compressed on his chest, her body gone limp. He kissed her again, then nuzzled at her neck. Vanessa sighed, closed her eyes, turning her head upward and away so he could languish there, inhaling her sweet perfume.

He whispered into her collar bone, "Get in. I'll start it up, put the heater on, and we'll snuggle a bit in the back."

She tensed.

"Please, Jeremy. I can't. This isn't right."

She heard herself say the words, but in her mind she knew she could and she knew it was.

And she knew she would, but not yet.

During the last few days, ever since the Christmas Eve fire on East 57th Street, something cloudy inside the fabric of Vanessa's being gradually had become clearer to her. She now understood that what had always been her subtle teasing, the veil of feigned shyness in her eyes, her deceptively staged vulnerability and apparent defenselessness, the way she carelessly dressed, nonchalantly leaving some buttons opened here, skirt and dress hems raised there, even the way she stood with Jeremy right now, at first tense and struggling, now so loose and relaxed offering her inviting smile and her body to him, all these were the powerful tools she always had used well to build anticipation, desire and need, bartering her coy mannerisms and sensual behavior in return for the attention, affection and love she craved during each and every encounter, when the man in her arms wanted to conquer her, to use her, to own her for the moment.

She stared up into Jeremy's hazel eyes and saw his passion. She knew that look. She'd seen it a hundred times. It was the overwrought struggle between obsession and frustration, like the looks of eagerly anticipatory prisoners caged in cinder block cells on death row just waiting for the telephone calls and their pardons from the governor.

"You need something, I can tell," she softly said to him.

"God yes, yes I do. Give it to me."

She embraced him, kissing him hard, reaching inside his coat to place her hand between his legs. She squeezed, gently.

He touched his nose to hers. "You get your skinny ass inside that van now, Van."

She hopped in.

He got in, threw her down on the bench seat, and began stripping her.

Vanessa felt him exploring every inch of her body with his strong hands. He lay on her. They were wrapped in a tangled embrace, his heavy body pressing her down, his moist lips kissing her breasts, his fingers feeling her wetness.

She pushed up on his stomach to give herself room to reach between his legs to open his pants and slide down his boxers.

Then she grabbed onto the hardest thing she had ever felt.

"Oh myyyyyy," she moaned, holding it, squeezing it, slowly rubbing it to feel every inch of its taut skin, the budding end of it, a bulbous mushroom, large and warm. She was consumed with passion for him. "Do me, Jeremy, do me."

He grabbed her legs to open them wider.

"No, no, not yet. Like this, like this."

She slid out from under him, got off the bench seat to rest on all fours on the floor of the van. She put her forearms on the carpeting, her head down, arching her back so her rear was high.

Then she reached around and slapped herself.

She spit out the words to him, "With your belt, your belt."

He frantically pulled his belt from the pants loops, coiling the buckle end around his hand a few times, then swung at her. The snap echoed inside the van like a rifle shot in a canyon.

"Ooohhh," she breathed, "oooooohhhhhhh. Again. Again."

He grabbed her hair, holding her head steady, then wielded the belt again. Snap. Again. Snap. Again. Snap. Snap.

Vanessa was drowning in a storm-tossed sea of pleasure and pain. She felt wetness beginning to seep down onto her thighs from between her legs.

Snap. Snap.

"Ummmpppfff," she screamed, "harder, harder!"

Sssnap. Sssssssnap. Sssssssssnap.

Then she cried out, "Enough, enough, enough!"

Sssnap. Sssssssnap.

He let go of her hair. She got up, pulling him over to the bench seat. He sat down. She straddled him, facing him, holding the back of his head, pulling his mouth to her chest, gingerly lowering herself onto his manhood, feeling it gradually opening her up as it slid slowly in.

14

August 1967
The Hudson Valley, New York

$\mathcal{T}$wenty-one, finally. I guess my body and me are legal everywhere now.

Last week, I had just finished the college summer session. I loved going to school here in the summers, starting right after I had graduated high school, and every summer since. For this term, I earned an A in Comparative Literature and a B in Shakespeare, The History Plays.

Officially, I now was a senior at the State University College at New Paltz, majoring in English liberal arts. By next May, I will need to take just six more courses in order to snatch what for so long has seemed to me to be three elusive golden rings: my diploma, my bachelor's degree, and my validation as a writer. All this from the gaping, Hydra-like jaws of the monster, this no-name State University college, with its myriad rules, regulations and idiosyncrasies, its mundane curricular and graduation requirements, its tedious loop-de-loops of requisites and prerequisites.

It has been worse than Daedalus' maze.

Scheduling was under the quarter system, which divided the regular academic year from late August to December, from January to early March, and then from late March to the middle of June.

So, for the rest of my college career, I would need only to take two courses during each of the remaining three quarters.

I thought then that I could do that with my eyes closed.

I was living in a small two-story house on Chestnut Street with Sherry O'Shea, a psychology major, and two other girls. Sherry was a tall skinny redhead from a farm in Pennsylvania, a sweet girl who had brought from home her favorite Barbie doll, which she fastened to one of her bedposts with duct tape, and a photograph of a pet cow named Bessie, which she had stuck to the wall above her bed with bubble gum. She always was homesick. She frequently and compulsively would borrow my clothes, soil them, and then, while I was in class, clandestinely drop them into my laundry basket when she was done with them. She and I shared one of the two bedrooms on the second floor of the old house.

In the other bedroom was Roseanne Abruzzi, an art major, a lusty, full-busted, fun-loving Italian girl from Albany, and Hadee Shah, a language major, a quiet, reserved, petite, exotically beautiful exchange student from Iran. The four of us had been renting the house together since our sophomore year, when campus dormitory life suddenly had become too restrictive and too confining for us.

What was with the idea that girls had a curfew then, and the boys didn't?

Anyway, we also liked beer, a lot, loud music and dancing, dust and disarray, staying up all night intending to do our work, but ending up having raucous pajama parties and marathon gab sessions, those and many other naughty transgressions and indiscretions which were scrutinized by and frowned upon every day and every night by Sara Ann Fardy. Sara was our one-hundred seventy-three pound, five-foot-three, Sumo-like Resident Assistant at Scudder Hall.

She was the law, and we were the perps.

The straw that broke the camel's back was the night of December 12th, about eighteen months ago. In our room at Scudder Hall that night, Sherry, Roseanne, Hadee and I were trying to study for finals. Hearing The Young Rascals singing "Good Lovin'" over and over again at an incredibly high decibel level, and the constant hissing of the radiators, which were pumping oppressive waves of heat into our small dormitory room, weren't much helping us to remain on task and to concentrate on what we knew we really should be doing.

It was a few minutes past 11:00 p.m., just after the time the girls' imaginary curfew bell had sounded, when Roseanne went to the window to open it a little for some fresh air. Her boobs got there five seconds before the rest of her did. She saw something, and then screamed, "Look at this! Will you look at this!"

Sherry, Hadee and I ran to the window. There below, huddled on the patio expanse in front of the entry doors to the dormitory, was a group of about a dozen boys from Bouton Hall. They were freezing, shivering from the cold. I saw one of them holding a guitar. I heard a strum. Then they all started singing "No Reply" by the Beatles. They sang, "This happened once before . . ."

They were wonderful, offering an impromptu concert of sorts for the girls at Scudder Hall. The boys' voices were a rough blend of discordance with some faint harmony, their warm breaths forming clouds around the words they were singing to us.

I heard other windows opening with fury, then giggles, cheers, and then kisses being blown.

I watched two boys in particular.

One was playing the guitar, a Gretsch I think it was, smiling and singing in the night. Even though it was bitter cold outside that evening, the fingers of his left hand were flying over the frets to form the chords needed to sing to. He was boyishly cute, though certainly not handsome. One of his two upper front teeth slightly lapped over the other, his curly black hair was long and thick, and he wore glasses with black frames. For a moment, I thought he was Buddy Holly, back from the dead.

The other boy I was staring at was standing next to him. That guy had his hands in the pockets of his Navy coat, a long green scarf coiled around his neck two or three times, its stringy ends brushing against his boot laces. He had wavy, reddish-brown hair, long sideburns, and a nose which looked two sizes too big for his face. But, he was cute, too.

I kept looking down at them. When they all finished singing, the two boys stood together in front while the others regrouped behind them for another song.

Something came over me.

I turned from the window and ran to my dresser. Now I heard them singing "I Ain't Gonna Eat Out My Heart Anymore." I fumbled in my drawer and found a pair of my black panties and a matching bra, grabbed them, and then ran back to the window.

During the nine seconds I was away from the window, Roseanne, the insatiable one, had wasted no time. She was breathing heavily. She excitedly said to me, "They're serenading us for the holidays. The one with the guitar is Super. The other one is The Rins. They're both really named Dennis." She was so pumped up. "I told them Room 219, Room 219, 219!"

I threw my bra out the window. The Rins picked it up, waving it to me. He tucked it into his jacket pocket. Then I threw my panty. Super stopped playing the guitar, hastily picked up my black undergarment, then put it on his head like a shower cap. He resumed playing, missing maybe only three bars. He looked so funny that the four of us just couldn't stop laughing.

Then, the boys behind him cried out, "More, more, more!"

Soon, an enormous assortment of dozens of pieces of lingerie, bras, panties, camisoles, corsets, slips, bustiers, tap pants, garter belts, girdles, stockings, merry widows, even pajamas, long johns and nighties, were in the air, a veritable snowstorm of cotton, silk, satin and flannel undergarments and bed clothes flurrying out from the open windows of Scudder Hall, landing like iron filings on the slate patio, the boys' hands the magnets. They quickly broke ranks and scurried to pick up everything.

Underwear is magic.

That night, after the serenading was over, the four of us realized we had to get out of the dormitory for good. Hadee went to her bed to study her notes, and Sherry lay down on the rug to read from a pendulous volume, *Abnormal Psychology*. Soon, they both were snoring.

Roseanne and I stayed awake for a while, gabbing on and on about the Dennises.

"God, Urse," she said, yawning with her arms wide open and pulled behind her, her braless breasts bulging like robust pineapples from under her tight t-shirt, "imagine what fun, you and me, with them?"

"Yes," I mused, thinking of something else.

In my mind, I couldn't stop fantasizing about my being alone with the two of them, and what they would do to me.

Soon after that night, in fact just before the beginning of the next quarter in January, we had moved off campus and ended up in the house on Chestnut Street. Sherry, Roseanne and I stayed there together for the next year. Regrettably, after only part of that semester, Hadee had to leave to do an internship at the United Nations in New York City. It was so sad to see her go, but I vowed I would keep in touch with her. I liked Hadee a lot. She was reserved, yet fun, and she always had a subtle grace and elegance about her, even during the thousand times or so when we were silly.

Anyway, with this summer session now over, I needed to focus my energies on two final tasks before the new recruits, the freshmen, arrived in nine days.

One was to start the planning and to begin making the preparations for the annual Beaux Arts Ball held in October, a sort of raunchy, uninhibited New Orleans Mardi Gras-style masquerade party, where all the weirdos, both students and faculty, dress up in costumes and masks and come out from under the rocks and from behind the woodwork for a night to let their inhibitions and their alter egos rise up from the ashes like a crazed flock of phoenixes suddenly brought to life.

The other was to get back to my part-time job as assistant editor of college publications.

My boss at school was Dean Mona Young, Ph.D., a massive, very masculine-looking woman at five-foot ten, the same height as I am, but at least seventy-five pounds heavier. The word around campus was that she was a flaming lesbian, but she never had made any advances toward me. At one-hundred fifteen pounds, I guess I was a little too insubstantial for her. Who knows?

I was in Dean Young's office, scanning through Pile A, the final drafts of the class lists, making sure for the powers that be that each course was filled to capacity for maximum profit and full room utilization. I was double-checking to see if there was a space, and then, and only then, was I to take a course request form from Pile B, the part-timers, commuters and audits, make a match, and then put someone's fanny into the empty seat.

When I thumbed through the English Department sheets, I saw the page for a Greek Mythology course. I carefully read it. Location, Main Building, Room 303. Time, Wednesdays and Fridays, 9:30 a.m. to 11:30 a.m. Credits, 3. Prerequisite, None. Seats, full. Instructor, D. Henry.

The blood stopped coursing through my veins.

I knew exactly where I would be on the morning of Wednesday, August 30, at 9:15 a.m. I would be in the Main Building, at the door to room 303, standing there, waiting, waiting, with my heart in my one hand and my soul in my other.

15

Sunday, December 31, 2000
Hoyt Street

Vanessa Fernandez lived in Brooklyn in a second floor apartment above an antique shop, less than half a block from Atlantic Avenue, one of the main thoroughfares in Carroll Gardens, a section of Brooklyn just a stone's throw from the Manhattan and Brooklyn Bridges, the Brooklyn Law School, and the old BHD, the infamous Brooklyn House of Detention, a prison which looms like something out of a Dickens novel. For the past few years, the neighborhood's commercial establishments have been teeming with regrowth, its residential properties with renovation. The old neighborhood's active revitalization is still in progress. The area is safe. It is clean. It is alive.

Her apartment was a modest place, but with two architectural anomalies. One was the bathroom. After opening her entry door from the landing, Vanessa needed only to take five short steps straight ahead through a narrow doorway to be standing directly in front of the toilet. The other was the two small bedrooms. They weren't really bedrooms, more like walk-in closets, seemingly added on as afterthoughts, one off the living room, the other off the kitchen.

The good thing was, if she made a hard left upon entering, her large living room, complete with fireplace and orderly courses of crimson brick from floor to ceiling, greeted her with warmth. A hard right, the large kitchen with a rectangular center counter. Her apartment was cozy, yet airy, with large windows in the living room facing Hoyt Street, and in the kitchen looking out back to a small yard overgrown with haphazard weeds, some piles of warped two-by-fours, and a round, above-ground swimming pool long abandoned, the little water still in it as thick and as green as split pea soup, its sides sagging as if it were about to implode.

Her apartment had character. It suited her fine.

She hopped out of the shower, toweled dry, then stood naked before the vanity, putting on makeup, just eyeliner and eye shadow, which is all she ever really needed.

She heard the phone ring from the kitchen.

Vanessa went to it and picked it up.

"Hello?"

"I just turned onto Hoyt. We'll be there in three minutes. Be ready."

She looked up at the clock on the wall.

"You and your shitty pickup truck," she said. Then she imitated his husky voice, "'We'll be there in three minutes.'"

She waited for a response. There was none.

Then she asked, "What's with the royal 'we'?"

He huffed. "You sassy bitch."

"Well, you're twenty minutes early," she said. "It's only ten after twelve."

"So? Somebody up there? Myers still breathing heavy after fucking you silly?" he asked.

"No, no one's here."

"Well then, what's your problem?"

"Nothing, Lieutenant," she said with a breathy tone, "it's just I guess your early afternoon bj will be a little longer than usual is all."

Vanessa loved playing Tony like a pinball machine.

"Bitch." He hung up.

Vanessa went to her bedroom. She put on black thigh high stockings, her black stilettos with ankle straps, a red thong bikini panty whose little lacy triangle patch in front barely covered what it was intended to cover, and a red, loose-fitting, silk camisole top.

Tony liked red and he liked black.

She looked in the mirror. She noticed how her breasts bulged from under the camisole causing it to ride up a little, like an awning on a patio, exposing a sliver of her stomach.

This'll do, she thought.

One knock at the door.

Vanessa went to it, closed her eyes, puckered her lips, then opened it.

Nothing happened.

She opened her eyes.

There was Lieutenant Tony Vly, leaning on the door jamb.

Next to him was Captain Tom Angola.

"Oh God, what's this?" she asked, suddenly feeling apprehensive and nervous.

"The royal We," he said slowly. "You'll see."

The men came into her apartment. She heard the door close behind them.

Tony knew to turn left toward the living room, but Tom had taken a few steps straight ahead.

Tony was on the couch. "I want a beer now, Van. Get it."

Tom was standing in the bathroom.

Vanessa looked at Tom. His eyes were paint rollers which already had traversed up and down every inch of her body a dozen times. His heavy breathing was commencing.

She looked back at Tony, then to Tom again.

Something came over her.

She put her fingertip to her lips and asked Tom, "And you, Sir, cervaza, too?"

Her accent. Music to his ears. "Sure, Nessa."

Something indeed had come over her.

Her anxiety was gone, replaced by anticipation, intrigue, expectation, passion and lust. She knew what they wanted to do to her, and she knew what she was going to do to make it so.

16

August 11, 1970
Schreiber's Lane, New Paltz

$\mathcal{I}$ had walked the three or four blocks from the Pine Funeral Home on Main Street in the village of New Paltz to the northern end of the State University campus. I wanted to be alone. I was thinking all along the way how nice the service had been, especially the flowers.

During the wake, I had heard the sounds of people's emotions, always the sounds, the sounds, their muffled sobs, their low, murmured moans of sorrow and condolences, the sounds of their clammy hands gently sliding in and out of mine, their breathy whispers of compassion for me, their tears tracking down their cheeks. All were lullabies of comfort to me.

I had wanted to be alone, and now, sadly, at twenty-four, I was.

David Henry lay dead.

I walked to the campus English department offices. They were located in a two-story, mostly ivy-covered building on the east side of the college's main quadrangle. I noticed a spot where some of the ivy angrily had been torn away, exposing a few courses of bricks on which I guess some disgruntled undergraduate English major had scribbled defiantly with chalk, To Lack Unity And Coherence Is To Be Free. I smiled.

I thought of David and his writing, and then said aloud, "No. No, it really isn't."

I kept on walking, across the quad with its lush grass and mature oak, sycamore and hickory trees, toward the Main Building, thinking that when I got there I would sit on one of the benches in the front of the doors on its right side, outside the entrance to the building which led into a small auditorium. I wanted to sit there and just bask awhile in the warm summer sun with my memories of David.

Sometimes, maybe you can go home again.

I was lost in thought when I heard a voice.

"Ursula, it's me."

My hearing always has been acute. When I was in elementary school, I always scored off the chart of every hearing test I had ever taken. Curiously, I also have perfect pitch. I can name a note when I hear it, like B-flat, D-sharp or whatever, even two at a time, three at a time, I think as many as six or seven, the name of each one, and the intervals in between. Too bad I can't sing. If I'm not excited or depressed, and just talking calmly and matter-of-factly, I speak mostly in and around the key of E-flat. Most people speak in the key of F. This typewriter I am using now types in the key of G-sharp.

Instantly I knew that voice from somewhere in my recent past. My mind, receiving the sounds of those three words from inside my ears—they had been spoken to me in the key of F-sharp—now was running a rapid, full-power scan through my friends-and-acquaintances data bank, searching for a match.

"Ursula," a pause, "it's me."

There, a match. I knew who it was.

Hadee Shah.

"Hadee! Hadee!" I screamed with joy.

I looked up and saw her. She was standing right in front of me. I had been so lost in thought about David that I hadn't processed the sounds of her footsteps coming toward me.

I jumped up. "Hadee," I said warmly, hugging her with

all my might, "the little Persian princess! How are you? How's things?"

She looked up, deep into my eyes. "I'm so sorry about David, Urse, really I am. I read the obituary in the paper three days ago on my way to work. I knew I had to drive up here from the city to be with you. I was on my way to stop by and pay my respects, but I knew I just couldn't do it. I'm so sorry, Urse, but deep down I just can't handle those things. So, I went to the Empire Market a little while ago to buy some flowers, thinking maybe I'd have a quiet service all by myself, maybe down at the bridge, and then throw them in the Wallkill River as a memorial of sorts for him, and for you, too. Anyway, I saw Dean Young in one of the aisles and she remembered me. She's still looks as lezzie as, well, you know, Urse."

We laughed.

"She and I chatted a bit and then she told me she had just come from David's service, and as far as she knew, you were headed this way. Here, I bought these for you."

She handed me a small bouquet of white carnations.

"Then I went by David's office and then came here."

I could see Hadee was very nervous, over-talking, her hands now wringing themselves tightly.

"If you weren't here," she said, "I was going to walk over to Scudder Hall, then drive back into town to our old house on Chestnut Street, figuring you might be there, and then, if you weren't, go out to your house on Schreiber's."

I took the flowers from her, sniffing them. "Thank you, Hadee, they're beautiful."

We reminisced for a long while, sitting there on the slate bench, basking in the sun, watching distraught freshmen coming and going, in and out of the side doors of the Main Building.

Finally, Hadee asked, "What happened, Urse?"

"Everything, Hadee," I said.

I closed my eyes for a moment. "Everything."

I was nervous now, too, and for some reason I just went on

and on, telling her my story, our story, David's and mine, beginning with those three wonderful, lovely and remarkable years in high school when I was David's student and he was my teacher.

"And then," I said, "after his dismissal of me in the end zone on graduation day, I went on with my life, thinking I would never see him again. But, I always carried a piece of him in my heart. Then, our paths crossed again, three years later. I remember I was right here, in this building, standing by the door to room 303, at 9:15 in the morning, on August 30, 1967. I had dressed appropriately for the occasion, a tight tube top, no bra—did we ever wear bras during our college days, Hadee?—a pair of your stringy, old, moth-eaten cut-off denim short-shorts you left behind when you went to the United Nations, your size 1, a tad smaller than my usual size 3, and platform shoes with four-inch heels, making me stand out like some girly obelisk at almost six-feet-two."

We both giggled again.

Then, my speech slowed a bit.

"Poor David, he was always so self-conscious about his height. Five-eight, tops, with his shoes on. Anyway, I was waiting in the hall by the door when some kids began walking past me into the room. I wanted to tell each of them about the magic which was in store for them in David's class. I looked at my watch. It was exactly 9:21. David was such a time freak, so I knew he wouldn't be late for his class. He hated to be late for anything. And then, I saw him coming from the elevator, as handsome to me and as adorable as ever. I remember that moment as if it happened five minutes ago, Hadee."

She put her arm around my shoulders.

"I saw him there, his disobedient hair still trying to release itself from his head, his black glasses, with those big bottle-bottom lenses, sliding down a little on his nose, his camel sports jacket, the black shirt, the dark brown slacks, the hush puppies. He loved those shoes. I wanted him so bad in that hallway, right then and right there. He was walking toward me while reading from a paperback book, Graves' *The Greek Myths*, lost in thought. He raised his head to locate the door to the room, his line of vision parallel to the floor, and then he looked up higher, right into my eyes. He stopped dead in his tracks. He blushed, then smiled at me, and for the first time that I noticed that he ever did, he slowly eyed me up and down, staring a moment longer at my legs, which he told me later seemed to him to stretch from my cute little fanny down to the floor, through it, and all the way to the snack bar in the basement of the building three floors below! He loved my legs so much, Hadee. Then, he came to me. 'Ursula, Ursula,' he said, standing almost tiptoe to kiss me on the cheek. I bent down a little so he could reach my face. 'Mr. Henry,' I said slowly and breathily, as an eager teenage groupie would on her knees at the feet of some swaggering, strutting, testosterone-laden rock star she adored. And, I then threw in more than my usual hint of sexual acquiescence and total body surrender."

"Ur-su-la!" Hadee said, "You're sooo naughty!"

"I know, I know. Anyway, he told me to meet him downtown later, at Barnaby's, for lunch. I couldn't wait for the time to pass. I was sitting in a booth when he arrived. He slid in, opposite me, and immediately said, 'I need you to do something for me, Ursula.' I rattled out, 'Anything, Mr. Henry, anything,' and I meant it. Then he slowly said the words I thought I was never, ever going to hear from him. 'Ursula, honey,' he said to me, 'I need you to be with me.' I was shocked."

I stared into Hadee's ebony eyes. She was so attentive, hanging on my every word.

I went on.

"He was hugging his glass with his hands then, seltzer with lemon, he just hated alcohol so much, staring at the lemon slice in it, breathing slowly, telling me his wife had died from leukemia almost two years ago. Then, he had to find a new life to try to ease his memories of her, quitting his job at the high school in Hicksville, and selling his house. He applied for college teaching positions to get away from the one thing he always had detested about public school kids, to him the constantly irritating and aggravating ways they could find to waste their time and their talents. He accepted a position here at New Paltz, then soon after bought an old farmhouse out on Schreiber's Lane, settling in on the perilous tasks of a new voyage, a little scared, and yet totally invigorated. He was writing a lot, finishing a book manuscript entitled *Rivers of Whispers, Stories of Knowing*, a collection of four pieces, a novella, *The Afterdeath of Ethan Bishop*, and three short stories, *All Fall Down, Morrison's Necklace*, and *The Arrangement*. He wanted me to be with him, Hadee, to live with him, to take care of him, to help him edit his book, which I did like a hundred times, and of course I said, 'Yes Mr. Henry, I mean David, yes, yes, I will.' Then, well, then I dropped out of college, moved in with him at the farmhouse, and even though there were no other women in his life then, at least that I was aware of, I willingly became his mistress, the way he wanted it, the dream I had had since I was fifteen finally come true."

I knew I was babbling, but I couldn't help it.

Hadee sensed this from me, saying, "No, no, Urse, it's okay, tell me. Tell me everything."

"Oh, Hadee, Hadee," I said, "he was so strong willed, just like a teacher, and he had such a defiant bravado in his ways to me, maybe trying to compensate for his height, who knows?"

I stared off across the quad at the English department building, my vision focusing on the small, second-floor window of David's now empty office. I was thinking about what I had just said to Hadee. It suddenly occurred to me that I never had told Hadee, or anyone else for that matter, about the way David had treated me.

For some reason, I now wanted Hadee to know. Maybe it

would be a way for me to release my sorrow and my frustrations. Maybe it would be a way for me to accept, by saying the words aloud, that our love affair, David's and mine, was now ended, irretrievably lost, and only glorious memories of sense and feeling.

And then I thought that if I say the words aloud, then maybe my memories will live on in me.

"Hadee," I said, composing myself to open my heart to her, "he was so strict with me, like I was still his student and he was still my teacher, so difficult at times, but I obeyed him, his every whim and wish, and in return he loved me to death, in bed consuming me and my body, opening me up to, well, you know, different things."

"I see," Hadee said quietly. She was getting uncomfortable. I went on anyway. I just had to.

"Sometimes he would tie me up, sometimes he'd discipline me, spanking me with his belt, sometimes he forced himself on me, so, well, I played along. I wanted to. I wanted to be what he wanted me to be. He liked being rough with me, making me do all the things a whore was expected to do for her John, but he always was loving to me afterwards, demanding, yet passionate, attentive in the heat of passion, although sometimes as distant as a stranger on the street, and then so kind to me, but sometimes in the throes of his lovemaking to me he could be so cruel to me, insisting that I accept the enthralling, all-consuming pleasure and pain he was giving to me."

I reached to touch her hand, whispering to her, "Hadee, he needed to own me in bed, like property. Something inside of me relished every minute of it and I knew that by letting him take me in those ways, and my giving myself totally to him, that he would love me so very, very much. And he did."

There, I had said the words aloud.

I sensed Hadee was backing off from me and from what I had just told her. She took a deep breath and exhaled.

"But, Urse, I mean, well, what actually happened?" she

asked me, changing the subject.

I exhaled slowly, too, feeling the tear ducts inside my eyes beginning to well.

"Your car's here, right, Hadee? Drive me to my car, it's still at the funeral home. Follow me out to the house and then we can talk more there, okay sweetie? Please?"

"Yes, of course, Urse."

She drove me back to town, neither of us speaking. While sitting in her car, I was daydreaming of my man, David Henry, my David, and I guess in her mind Hadee was trying to understand some of the things I had said to her at the bench about David's lovemaking. I could sense she was still struggling with them.

At the funeral home, I got in my car, drove off, and Hadee followed me.

The ride from town on Route 32 seemed so much longer this time. Finally, we made our left turns onto Schreiber's Lane. We got to the house.

When Hadee and I stepped inside, I felt weak. I heard the silence, the dreadful, overbearing, weighty, oppressive, thick-in-the-air silence: no sounds of David relentlessly punching his typewriter keys into a coma as he feverishly worked on his writing, no long slurping sounds as he drank from his numberless cups of black coffee, no sounds of him puffing away on his Marlboros, no sounds of his red pen scribbling across his students' papers making his comments and corrections in a handwriting which was so bad and nearly so indecipherable that most of the kids couldn't read what he had written, most of them so puzzled by the scratchings they just assumed he wrote them in Swedish or Chinese.

Then, I looked up at the living room ceiling, just below our bedroom.

More silence.

No sounds of his moaning as I was playing with him, no sounds of my heavenly, delirious gasping, grunting and screaming with pleasure and in pain as I was succumbing to him, surrendering to him, acting out all his fantasies for him.

He had been my teacher in so many ways.

Hadee sat down at the kitchen table.

"Something to eat, Hadee? A drink?" I asked her.

"No, Urse, thanks. Just tell me what happened."

I sat down next to her.

"We were in bed, sleeping," I told her, "and I was dreaming this same dream that always comes to me, frequently, maybe every three months or so, the same one I've had over and over again since I was six or seven. I'm in the middle of the woods near my parents' house at night, sitting down and leaning my back against the stump of a dead cherry tree, and then all of a sudden I feel someone with strong hands lifting me up and in an instant I'm naked, teetering on the top of the stump, desperately trying to hold on, and there are dozens of people hiding in and among the weeds, their eyes staring at me, watching me. Oh, Hadee, it's so humiliating. And then at the end of my dream, I fall off the stump. It always wakes me up. I woke up then. I sat up in bed, sweating, my heart thumping away. I reached over for David to touch him, but he wasn't there next to me."

I was crying then, weeping uncontrollably, like a child who had lost her puppy, hearing the sounds of my teardrops splashing on the kitchen table like plump raindrops on a windshield during a heavy storm.

"It's okay, Urse," Hadee said, holding my hands in hers.

I settled myself.

"So I got out of bed, thinking David might be downstairs in the den typing, but I didn't hear the typewriter keys. Just before I walked out of the bedroom to go down to look for him, I saw something in my peripheral vision. David was lying on the floor at his side of the bed. He had fallen out. Maybe that's what had startled me, making me wake up. I rushed over to him, knelt beside him, feeling his chest, but he wasn't breathing. He was just dead, Hadee, dead, dead, dead."

She was crying now, too.

"A stroke, Hadee. He had a massive stroke."

17

Monday, January 1, 2001
Manhattan

Early yesterday afternoon, several of the firefighters, Vanessa Fernandez, Jeremy Myers, and three others, coincidentally had called in sick. Vanessa had gotten up about noon, as she usually does when she's going to work, made her sick call, then went back to bed. She slept soundly, waking around 9:00 p.m., deciding that she would go to Fiore's in Manhattan to spend the special New Year's Eve there. This was the big one, the real Millennium.

She really didn't have any other place to go.

Fiore's hadn't been crowded this Eve, maybe a dozen or so of the regulars and a handful of newcomers, all men. There was quiet conversation among them about women, college and professional football and basketball, the stock market, auld lang syne and all of that, the Yankees and their winter trades and acquisitions, and women.

There were the sounds of ice shards clinking into glasses, wooden stick matches being struck then bursting into flames with hisses to light cigarettes, salty peanuts being rustled up from aluminum trays by hungry hands, and Tony Bennett sweetly crooning "Night and Day" from the jukebox.

James Russert was punching the cigarette machine trying to retrieve his five dollars in quarters when, from behind him, he heard a sudden chorus of squeals and whistles. His back was turned, so he didn't know what had caused it.

He looked over his shoulder.

He saw a goddess.

"Jesus," he said under his breath.

A young woman had sauntered in, stopping in the small foyer, throwing kisses to the men on barstools. They had just as eagerly greeted her, catching the kisses from her. She took a few steps forward, the sway in her hips pronounced, tossing her leather bolero jacket over to old man Fiore, the bartender.

James Russert stared at her.

The woman was wearing high heels, really high heels, black stockings, a dark gray, flared, herring bone mini skirt that looked like it belonged to her teenaged sister, and an oppressively tight, long-sleeved, black, V-neck top, the shiny, part-cotton, part-spandex fabric pulling across her chest from every direction stretching the trim V of the neckline into a portly U.

No bra.

Now she was standing next to and talking with an old bald guy who was seated at the bar.

Russert saw Fiore hang up the woman's jacket. Then the bartender went over to her.

Vanessa didn't care for the specialty of the house, dark ale, and so without asking Fiore served her her liking, a glass of chilled Colombard, with a seltzer and lemon chaser, no ice.

James Russert slowly walked toward the woman, deciding he would position himself to the right of the man on the barstool, the woman was on the bald guy's left, so as not to appear too obvious.

As James reached the bar, Fiore asked him, "Another, pal?"

He said, "Yes, bourbon, please."

Russert was looking straight ahead, his eyes glued to the mirror behind the bar, watching the woman's reflection.

Fiore brought the bourbon.

James overheard the bald guy talking to her. He was commenting on the woman's outfit.

"Nice, Van, real nice clothes." Then, "You got great legs on you, honey. You're such a little hottie," he was telling her.

"Thanks, Douglas," she said, "you're so sweet to me, but it's these damned stockings."

From the corner of his eye, James watched as the woman pinched both sides of her skirt hem with her thumbs and forefingers and then lifted it up above her waist, holding it there as if she had just unveiled a statue. Russert focused his peripheral vision on the woman's long, shapely legs, the bold black stripes of the stockings' tops, a stressed garter attached to each, the tops perfectly perpendicular to her thighs, and then to that little delta, that wondrous, triangular meeting place, that Shangri-la, where her thighs met her lacy panty, right between her legs.

"They keep sliding down," he heard her say to the bald guy, who had regained his balance after nearly falling off his stool to look down at the display, "so I have to use garters all the time."

Douglas moaned.

So did James.

The woman heard both moans.

"Hi there, I'm Vanessa," she said, leaning in a bit over the bald guy's lap to direct her words to James. She was still holding her skirt hem above her waist with her fingertips.

James turned to his left. He was staring at her delta, which then suddenly disappeared.

Vanessa had let go of her skirt.

He looked up, smiling at her. "Hey you. Russert. James Russert."

Exactly fifty-four minutes later, at twelve minutes to midnight, on the true Millennium New Year's Eve, Vanessa Fernandez was in James Russert's hotel room.

Vanessa liked James Russert right away.

He was well-dressed.

Nice pin-striped suit, she had thought when she first saw him, and he's tall—Vanessa loved tall men—and boyishly cute, a little older than me, but, well, what the hell?

Vanessa noticed he had a peculiar way of speaking, always animated, with a slight, very slight affectation in his speech, not really a lisp, and he sometimes drawled, but only in passing over certain words, casually, not persistently like a born-and-bred Southerner. His brown eyes were inviting, and his smile enchanting.

I like you, James Russert, she had thought.

James playfully had thrown Vanessa on the bed. She lay on her back with her legs open, her skirt gathered at her waist, one hand sheathed behind her head buried in her hair, the other holding onto the side edge of the mattress. Standing at the foot of the bed, James was staring down at her, at her Shangri-la. His mind was momentarily transforming her into a thick wedge of a three-tiered, chocolate-covered, custard-filled cake topped with generous dollops of sweet whipped cream, a decadent dessert waiting to be licked, savored, then gingerly tasted, savored again, and then ravenously devoured.

"It'll be the new year soon," she said calmly, while he was frantically busy stripping her.

She knew what was coming.

"Yes, I know, babycakes, I know."

There, she was naked.

"Well, Jimmy, Jimmy, Jimmy," she said demurely, "now are you gonna gimmie, gimmie, gimmie?"

He gave.

And good.

At dawn, Vanessa woke up, seeing Jimmy Russert lying next to her in the bed, unconscious and obviously exhausted from making love to her through the night. She sidled out of the bed, then started to get dressed. Snapping her garters to her stockings, Vanessa heard her voice inside her head, I like you a lot, Jimmy Russert.

Finishing dressing, she whispered, "Men, they love to look, they just love to look. And touch. And feel. And you're no different, Jimmy Russert."

Of course she knew he had been staring at her in the mirror last night. She was alone, he was alone, and it was a holiday. What better way to get something started, she had thought then, then to show garters and stockings?

Underwear is magic, absolute magic.

She put on her bolero jacket, left the room, and then went back to her apartment in Brooklyn to sleep in her own bed, alone.

Later, at 3:50 p.m., Vanessa was at the firehouse, hurriedly on her way up the stairs to the locker room when she suddenly sensed something strange in the air, something which just didn't belong, like the smell of rotting mulch in a bakery, the odor of skunk at a wedding, the sounds of uncontrollable laughter in a cemetery, the deafening noise from a phalanx of jet fighters soaring through a child's bedroom at night. It was something so out of place that it startled her deep down to the buried nerves inside her spine.

She felt damp chills mousing through her body.

Then she realized it was the aura of death.

On the landing above, Jerry D'Amato and Ed Heinz were talking to each other with looks of sadness and grief on their faces, with tones of disbelief, sorrow and pity in their voices.

Vanessa knew something terrible had happened.

She rushed up to the small landing, then squeezed herself in between Jerry and Ed.

"¿Qué pasó?" she asked, without thinking which language she was speaking. Then, "I mean, What's going on? What happened?"

They looked at her tentatively. "It's Jeremy," Ed said.

"What?" A pause. "What? Tell me, tell me," she said directly.

"Seems last night he and his wife and his kid were on their way home from her mother's in Jersey. They had stopped over for an early dinner and then started back before the traffic picked up for New Year's Eve and all. They came out of the tunnel and a few blocks later were clipped in an intersection, two drunk women joy riding in a Mustang, thinking they could rocket through against a red light," Ed said.

"And? And?" Vanessa demanded, holding her breath.

Jerry said the words to her. "She's dead. The little one, too. Strapped in the car seat, but it didn't matter. The van was totaled. Jeremy's at St. Luke's, you know, across town, West side on Tenth, not too bad. They're doing some tests. Holding him for observation. He'll be fine."

Jerry stopped, exhaling loudly. "Well, you know what I mean."

New Year's Eve.

The end of something, the beginning of something.

Transition.

It seems at every crossroad destiny always has a hand.

Vanessa looked at Jerry, then to Ed. For an instant, something inside her, the sense of denial, forced her to put aside the seriousness of the moment. She was thinking about what had happened to her last night, how she had hooked up with Jimmy Russert at Fiore's and then ended up in his hotel room. She also was thinking about what fun it would have been to be with her regular men, Tony and Tom, and Jeremy, too, any one of them, or all three. She remembered getting dressed to go to Fiore's, daydreaming for a while then about the three of them, but stoically accepting the fact that none of them could be with her. Tony has a wife. It's a holiday. Jeremy's married, with child. Even Tom Angola couldn't. Married, three children.

Coming around from her strange reverie, she whispered, "And now, this. This. Jeremy's wife and son, dead. Poor Jeremy."

She looked at Ed and Jerry. "They said he'll be okay?"

She didn't wait for either of them to answer.

She snapped at them. "Tell the Captain I'm going to be out a few days. I'll call in when I'm ready to come back."

Distraught, Vanessa ran from the landing, down the stairs, outside the firehouse, straight to her '78 Corvette.

18

August 1973
Schreiber's Lane

$\mathcal{A}$t twenty-seven, I still couldn't understand the difference between being rich and being wealthy, even though I know someone once had said that being rich allows you to chose the roadways for your car of destiny to travel on, but being wealthy allows you to drive. So be it.

Fourteen months ago, one of David's stories from his book *Rivers of Whispers, Stories of Knowing*, the novella, *The Afterdeath of Ethan Bishop*, had been made into a movie called *Darkness and Light*, starring Al Pacino in the lead role. Pacino had given a tremendous performance, later earning an Oscar nomination, but he didn't win. Although I truly admired David's fantastical tale of mythological monsters and a lonely, heartbroken man who travels to the other side, I really never thought it had enough mettle to carry itself from the printed page to the silver screen.

I was wrong. It was wonderful.

This movie business had happened so fast.

Modest royalty checks from David's book had been dribbling in, and then, all of a sudden, big, fat residual checks from the movie started filling my mailbox to its brim.

I guess I'm wealthy.

David had been dead almost two years then. I regret in my

heart of hearts that he hadn't lived long enough to see the admiration and the respect for his writing grow.

I remember I was mowing the front lawn with an old push mower we had when fate intervened in my life, again.

I was lost in thought, traversing the lawn, reminiscing about how David used to like to sit on our porch, sucking on a straw from a glass filled with iced tea, no sugar, while he was scribbling in his marble composition book. At regular intervals, he would look up from his page to watch me struggling with the mower. When he told me it was time to cut the grass, he always made me wear short-shorts and a skimpy top, or sometimes just my bikini. And even though I thought it was a little dangerous for me, I also had to be barefoot. I always did what David told me to do. He said it turned him on to see me that way.

Of course I did all the chores around the house. A few weeks into our relationship, David had promoted me from being his mistress to being his whore—I really never understood the distinction—and he had expected me to do everything. I had wanted him to promote me from his mistress to his wife, but he did not care to discuss it. I never pressed him about this.

Looking back, maybe the mistress-to-whore thing was really a demotion of sorts, but it really didn't matter to me. I wanted him to be happy. David always knew what was best for me. I was happy. He owned me in every way. I knew my place with him. I devoted myself and all my energies to him. I loved him very much. I always have, ever since I was fifteen. I still do, with all my heart. I think of him each and every day. I miss him so very much.

Anyway, I was just about finished with the grass when I saw a late-model Cadillac Fleetwood Brougham coming up the road from Route 32. It coasted into our driveway. It was long and black, very black. It reminded me of a hearse.

I was thinking, Now what?

The driver got out, then went around and opened the passenger side door. Two men exited, stretching their legs, waving their arms to clear the dust clouds which still were lingering. One of them walked toward me.

"Morning, Miss Ransom. Bill Kaufman, LoneStar Literary Agency."

The driver and the other man got back in the car.

Mr. Kaufman looked about fifty. He was short. Come to think of it, I've always loved being around short, older men for some reason.

Standing barefoot, I saw that I was almost two inches taller than he was. He was clean shaven, with thinning salt and pepper hair. He had a birthmark on the left side of his chin, a dark, pear-shaped blotch, maybe the size of a small diamond in an engagement ring, which looked to me like a housefly was resting right there on his face. In a way, I thought Mr. Kaufman was, well, sexy.

He came up to me, staring me up and down, looking at my short-shorts and my tube top, which is all I had on at the time.

"Miss Ransom, I'm here today to make you a rich woman."

"Really?" I asked him. "And how's that?"

David had told me a thousand times to be suspicious of men, especially the ones who stared at me up and down. All men are voyeurs, he had said, and they crave to touch, to feel, and then to ravage the all of what they see.

Mr. Kaufman handed me his card.

So far, so good.

We went into the house. Mr. Kaufman sat down on the couch in the living room. I sat directly across from him in David's favorite chair, an old, dark brown leather recliner. It was cold to the touch.

From his blazer pocket, Mr. Kaufman removed a sheaf of papers and placed them on the coffee table.

"Miss Ransom, I want you to—"

I interrupted him. "Ursula."

"Yes, yes, of course, of course. Ursula. Ursula."

He didn't know what to make of me just then, although I saw that he knew enough to stare between my legs for a moment. I now realized that when I had sat down, I had carelessly opened them. Now I closed them. He quickly raised his eyes to mine.

His friendly tone suddenly changed to one which was patronizing and dripping with condescension.

"This is business, Ursula, so I hope you'll understand. I represent your late husband's, I mean your late partner's literary interests at LoneStar. I think you know that during the three years or so since his book was published, sales of it have been tepid at best, but now there's been a promising new development."

I didn't say anything.

Mr. Kaufman went on.

"A famous actor that I think you might know from the movies recently read David's book while vacationing in France. He loved all of it. His agent contacted us. His agent wants to buy the rights for the Ethan Bishop story from us to make a film of it."

I didn't like Mr. Kaufman anymore, housefly on his chin and his shortness notwithstanding.

I thought for a moment.

I thought about the 'This is business, Ursula,' and the 'I hope you'll understand,' and the 'I think you might know,' and the 'buy them from us.'

"I see," I said.

I knew David had sold only the first-time publication rights of his book to LoneStar. He had told me his book was his child and that he never would relinquish parenthood. For David, adoption by LoneStar was out of the question. I understood his metaphor. He didn't have his own literary agent or his own attorney then, so after his manuscript had been accepted for publication, David agreed with LoneStar to the standard, constrictive, you're-nothing-without-us royalty contract for new authors, but before he signed it, he vehemently insisted that a first-time rights rider be included in order to protect his baby. What he wanted was to have LoneStar in charge only as far as the publication of the first edition of the book itself was concerned. Anything after that, the second edition, paperbacks, inclusion in anthologies and so on, David had told me, was ours.

"And?" I asked Mr. Kaufman.

"We're prepared to offer you a lump sum payment of fifty-thousand dollars up front, and a residual of one-percent of the movie's net."

"I see," I said.

I had a strange reverie then. I remembered the time when David and I had gone to Sears to return something, I've forgotten what, and we didn't have a receipt. There was a nice looking man behind the returns counter. David handed me whatever it was we were bringing back and told me to undo three of my blouse buttons, saunter up to the counter, arch my back, smile, bat my eyelashes, and speak slowly, deeply, with breaths in between my words. I didn't think I could do that, but with David's coaching and insistence, I did. I always obeyed David. After a few moments of banter, the returns man eagerly handed me a credit slip, no questions asked.

David had told me I sometimes had a power over him. I thought he was joking when he said that to me. I had many things with David, but I never believed power over him was one of them. He told me I was wrong. He said I had a way about me that screamed a femininity, a vulnerability, a sensuality, which, as a lusting hunter of our species, he gravitated to, desired and craved.

I had understood his metaphor that time, too.

He knew he would have had a difficult time returning the item, but he told me I wouldn't. He was so right.

Something now came over me.

I had a hunter, Mr. Kaufman, sitting across from me, a lowly gatherer of the species, who wanted now to screw me, figuratively speaking. And, maybe literally, too.

I decided quickly that I would have neither.

I opened my legs wide now, pointing my feet inwardly so I was pigeon-toed, placed both my hands on the top of my head, laced my fingers through my hair, and arched my back.

"And what do I have to do for you to get all that for me?" I asked him in an agonizingly slow stream of pouty breaths.

He smiled. When he did, his housefly seemed to move a

little closer to his mouth. I was hoping it would buzz in.

He pushed his sheaf of papers to the edge of the coffee table toward me. "Just sign here on the dotted line, Ursula."

I was nervous. I kept thinking of David and his child.

Again, something came over me.

I said the words.

"Three-hundred thousand up front, and six percent," a long pause, "of the gross. My David and I want to be paid before everyone else is."

I liked the sound of three and multiples of it.

"Miss Ransom, Miss Ransom!" he gasped, "I'm not authorized to broker a deal like that!"

He was so astonished a tall, skinny gatherer like me could be so brazen to a hunter like him. And savvy, too.

"Miss Ransom," he argued, "that's absolutely outrageous given the tentativeness of this business. We're not talking here about *Exodus* or *Peyton Place*, you know."

"Well then," I said, unwinding from my awkward pose, standing, and then walking toward the door, "just tell the famous actor *whom*," I sarcastically emphasized the word, "you think I might know that you failed to close the deal."

I was shaking.

Mr. Kaufman picked up his sheaf of papers from the coffee table, put them back into his blazer pocket, got up, and then came toward me. He was staring at me up and down again.

At the door, he stopped in front of me.

He looked up into my eyes and said coldly, "I know you know what you just did, but I don't think you know what it means."

I smiled down at him. "I'll take my chances with the actor's ego. You know, Bill, the one *whom*," more emphasis, "you think I might know."

He walked out of my house and then got into the car. It drove away.

Fifteen days later, I'm having dinner in New York City with three men, a penitent and remorseful Mr. Kaufman, Steven Lind,

Al Pacino's agent, and Peter Thaler, a rep from Paramount Pictures.

David would have been so proud of me.

I settled for three-hundred thousand up front, and three percent of the movie's gross.

For so many reasons, the number three has come to mean so much to me in my life.

The film opened to rave reviews and sellout crowds. It topped the earnings chart for six weeks in a row.

My first residual check was for one-hundred, sixty-five thousand dollars.

Ever since then, the checks have been coming in about once every three weeks.

I knew I had done the right thing for my David, and for his baby, too.

19

Tuesday, January 2, 2001
Manhattan

When Vanessa had rushed from the firehouse, she thought at first she would go straight to St. Luke's Hospital to see Jeremy.

Instead, she went home.

She had managed to calm herself while driving. She carefully drove downtown through the crowded city streets, then over the Brooklyn Bridge to Atlantic Avenue. All the way, her mind was active, thinking about what had happened to Jeremy, to his wife and to his son, but she had kept her emotions in check.

When she got to Hoyt Street, she didn't bother to look for a parking space. At the corner, she drove her 'Vette up onto the sidewalk, narrowly missing a fire hydrant, then creeped a little farther to the front of the antique shop, stopping parallel to the doors to the stairs to her apartment.

She hopped out, ran inside, then up the stairs.

As she was fumbling in her purse for the key to her door, she heard a voice from above.

"Van? Van? Is that you?"

She punched the key into the lock and turned it.

"Yes, Bren," she said, "it's me."

Brenda Villanueva came down the stairs from her third floor apartment. Vanessa already had gone inside her own.

Brenda went in. She found Vanessa in her bedroom. She saw Vanessa rampaging through the dresser drawers.

"Van, what's up? What you doing here now, girl, no work today?"

Vanessa said the words in Spanish. "Dios mío, Jeremy tuvo un accidente. Su esposa esta muerta y su hijo esta muerto tambien."

Vanessa hurriedly crammed her backpack.

"Oh God!" Brenda screamed in English, crossing herself above her chest. "An accident? His wife dead? His baby? How did it happen? Is Jeremy okay?"

Vanessa finished packing several pairs of panties, two pairs of jeans, some socks, and four camisole tops. Then she quickly brushed past Brenda to get her toothbrush, deodorant, some perfume, and her eye liner from the bathroom.

"Yes, yes, he's okay, still in the hospital though, and I'm going there right now as soon as I'm done here."

She threw her toiletries into her backpack and then headed for the door.

Brenda opened it for her. They went out onto the landing.

"I don't know when I'll be back, Bren." She locked the door.

They hugged.

Brenda looked into Vanessa's eyes. "It's okay, babydoll, I understand. You call me if I can do anything, if you need anything, anything. Promise?"

They kissed each other on the lips.

"Thanks, Bren. I will."

Vanessa arrived at the hospital at 8:40 p.m., parking on Tenth Avenue. She got out of her car and purposefully walked straight to the entrance doors.

Pushing through, Vanessa rushed to the information desk in the lobby to ask the attendant seated there for Jeremy Myers' room number. After doing so, she impatiently looked away, hearing a clock ticking in her head as the woman shuffled through dozens of index cards in a metal box on the desk.

Realizing that too many things, most of them unsettling, were flashing through her mind, Vanessa soon turned back to watch the attendant in order to try to focus on something tangible, but she couldn't quite free herself from her overdrive of thoughts. Jeremy's wife. His son. Jeremy. Jeremy's infidelity. Her guilt.

Now staring harder at the seated older woman, Vanessa observed her trying to do her best to find the right card. She noticed the woman's hair, a perfectly even blend of strawberry blonde and streaks of dark gray, her short-sleeved silk blouse, her skinny arms, the woman's long, thin fingers, no wedding ring, her impeccably manicured nails rapidly flipping through the cards.

Finally, the woman said, "Sorry this is taking me so long, but I volunteer to do this only a couple of nights a week and sometimes I get, oh, never mind. Okay, here it is, Myers, with an M and a Y. Jeremy. Room 219. I'm sorry, but there's no visitor access upstairs until eight o'clock tomorrow morning."

"Please, ma'am, please, I need to see him now," Vanessa begged, "please."

Their eyes met and held.

The seated woman could see the longing in Vanessa's facial expression and could hear the passion of need straining in her voice. The woman felt something for the young Spanish girl and understood the urgency and desperation in her request.

"I'm sorry," said the woman, "but let me ask the security guard over there," she pointed, "if we can make an exception this one time, okay?"

"Thank you, thank you," Vanessa said.

The attendant rose to go to the security guard who was stationed near the bank of elevators.

The guard and the woman whispered for a few moments.

Then the woman returned to her seat at the desk as the guard approached Vanessa.

Vanessa saw that he was muscular and trim. She smiled at him as he came closer to her.

He didn't smile back.

Shifting her weight to one leg and bringing the index finger of her right hand to her lips, Vanessa said her words softly and slowly, staring at the man's mouth as she spoke, not into his eyes.

"Please sir, I need to see Jeremy right away, and I won't stay long, just a few moments, I promise, cross my heart."

She then brought her index finger from her lips to her breast, pressing it there, slowly imaging an X as she inched her chest forward.

The security guard stared at her, taking in the coquettish way in which she stood and the erotic way in which she dragged her fingernail across her breast, but it was the coyness in her voice which, she thought, seemed to soften him.

At last, he smiled. Vanessa returned the expression eagerly.

"Save it, missy, I'm gay."

"Damn," she pouted.

Then he asked, "You his wife?"

Vanessa swallowed hard.

"No, no, I'm not."

"Sorry," the attendant said, "access denied."

He walked away from her to return to his post at the elevators.

As he passed by the information desk, Vanessa heard the guard say to the woman, "No one upstairs, Linda, it's well after eight now."

Vanessa found a chair for herself in the lobby, fell into it, then closed her eyes. Though her mind was still busy, she soon drifted off.

The sounds of murmured voices, the hustle and bustle of

footsteps, and a squeaky wheel on a supply cart being pushed by an orderly woke her.

She looked at her watch. 8:25.

"For Christ's sake," she whispered to herself.

She grabbed her backpack. She sidled through a mass of waiting visitors at the information desk, looking over the shoulders of the people crowded there. The older woman from last night had been replaced by a candy striper. Vanessa turned on tiptoes to see the bank of elevators. Oddly, there was no security guard there now.

Vanessa decided she would go directly to the elevators and then to room 219.

In the room, Jeremy was standing by the window, dressed in street clothes, talking to an older woman. It seemed as if they were trying to console each other, but with little success.

Vanessa walked in.

Hearing her enter, they turned to her.

Jeremy saw her.

"Vanessa. Vanessa, this is Lucille Barnes, my mother-in-law," Jeremy said, his voice a monotone, devoid of inflection. "Lucille, Vanessa Fernandez. She's in my unit."

The women exchanged uneasy smiles.

Vanessa asked, "Jeremy, are you okay? I mean, I mean, how are you feeling?"

No answer.

Another awkward moment.

Kissing Jeremy on his cheek, Lucille said, "I'm going now, Jeremy. Call me later. We need to make the arrangements."

Then she left the room.

Vanessa went to him, embracing him as a sister would her brother. She lay her head on his shoulder.

"I'm so sorry, so, so sorry, Jeremy," she said with genuine empathy in her voice.

"Thanks, Van, thanks," he whispered.

She looked up into his hazel eyes. They were reddened and seemed painted over with milk.

"Are you leaving now? It's okay for you to go? They discharged you?"

"Yep, I'm outta here."

Vanessa said, "You know I'm taking you home, right?"

"I know," Jeremy said. "Yes, I know."

20

September 1976
New Paltz

$\mathcal{I}$ remember I was so jittery almost that entire day because it was another time for me to try to go home again.

All afternoon I felt as if I was behind stage curtains, anxiously waiting for them to open, fearfully waiting to appear before an expectant crowd of hundreds, nervously waiting to act in a play on opening night. And then, I suddenly realized, at the very last moment, the instant before the curtains were about to be drawn open and I was to make my entrance, that I had forgotten all my lines.

I had parked my car in the little circle in front of the Main Building. I got out, locked the door, and then just stood there looking up at the imposing building for the first time in I don't know how long.

Pigeons were cooing on ledges.

There it was again, this special place where my dreams as a teenager and of a lifetime miraculously had been realized, my Shangri-la, where I had seen David as he was walking to his class, the time when I thought my heart literally would burst within my chest.

I really do know how long it has been.

Six years.

I was a college student again, this time at thirty years of age.

I had signed up for a French I class. This was the time in my life when I desperately wanted to learn to speak the language. For David. Sometimes during our lovemaking, he would yell at me in French, and, of course, I didn't understand him, I didn't know what he was saying, I didn't know what he wanted me to do, and I didn't know what he wanted from me. My ignorance and confusion only made him stir with a greater passion. Now, finally, I felt it was time to connect with him again and to hold onto another memory I had of him, no matter how inconsequential, no matter how silly.

I went to the classroom, sat down, opened my notebook and readied my pen. I looked around. There were seven people already seated.

Just great, I thought, there's only eight of us, it's going to be difficult for me to hide from recitations.

I was thumbing through the pages of my text when I heard someone come in and sit down next to me.

That makes nine, I thought.

"Hi there, Marianne Zahn, but everyone calls me Minnie."

I turned to look at her. Right away I got the impression she was friendly. She was smiling at me, a wide, warm, inviting smile. I noticed her perfectly straight and perfectly white teeth. Her long hair was perfectly straight, a streaking mix of light and dark browns. The bangs across her forehead were perfectly straight, too. She reminded me of Mary, from the singing group Peter, Paul and Mary, only thinner, more beautiful, and I really don't know why I thought this at the time, sexier, too.

"Hi, Marianne. Ursula. Ursula Ransom," I tried to say perfectly.

"Minnie, okay?" she asked.

"Oui, oui," I said, "Mademoiselle Minnie."

We giggled.

After class was over, we decided to go downstairs to the snack room in the basement of the building. The hallways were crowded at times, so I often was pushed behind her. I noticed there was something in her walk, the way her feet moved, her legs, her butt, her hips, her back, her arms, her neck, her head, her hair. There seemed to me to be, oh I don't know, a fluidity about her in the manner in which she carried herself, like the way an endless row of dominoes falls in an orderly stream of continuous motion.

We sat down in the snack room.

She asked me, "Did you get what she was saying," she was referring to our instructor, "about French culture, geography, literature, history? Geez, I mean all I want to do is to be able to talk dirty to my boyfriend."

I laughed. She was funny.

We talked for a while and then realized, simultaneously, that it was time for us to go.

We gathered our things.

"You live in New Paltz, Minnie?" I asked.

"No," she answered, "New Windsor. Just past Newburgh. Maybe twenty, twenty-five minutes from here."

"Right," I said. Then, "Want to stop by at my place for an early dinner? It's on your way."

"Why thank you, Ursula. Sure," she said, "no, no, I mean oui, oui, Mademoiselle Ursula."

We smiled at each other.

We went to our cars.

She followed me to my house.

We went in.

"This is beautiful, Ursula," she said, looking around the living room. "Just beautiful. I love the fireplace."

"Thanks, Minnie. My David decorated the place, and it had to be just so, and he liked—"

She piped in, "David? Where is he?"

"He's dead."

"I'm sorry, Ursula, so, so sorry, really I am," she said with genuine condolence in her voice.

It was then that I noticed that when she spoke, Minnie's

lips seemed to lag a moment behind her words, like what happens in a dubbed movie. I thought it was, well, I guess sensual in a way, her lips pouting slightly when she said words with soft consonants. They seemed to lazily drift out from her mouth.

"It's okay, Minnie. Thank you. Life goes on."

I insisted Minnie sit at the kitchen table while I spruced some leftover lasagna, made a salad, and sliced some Italian bread. We talked about nothing really, but as the minutes went by, I felt close to her, as if we had known each other a long time.

Dinner was ready. I brought some Colombard to the table. We began eating.

"You still miss him, don't you?" she asked.

"Yes," I said, "yes. Very much. It's been a long time."

After dinner, we picked up our glasses and the half-finished bottle of wine to go outside to sit on the front porch and relish the dusk. Neither of us had realized it already had started raining. It was pouring mercilessly.

We looked at our cars in the driveway.

All told, eight windows were open.

We rushed into the downpour, closed them, then shook ourselves off like dogs when we got back to the porch. We were drenched and cold.

"I'm soaked," she said.

"Me, too!" I said. "Let's go upstairs and see if we can find some dry clothes, then we'll come back down and I'll make a fire."

We went upstairs into the bedroom.

I opened the closet and got some things for us, a long, light-flannel nightgown for me, my favorite for lounging in front of the fireplace, and a fleece jogging outfit for Minnie.

Then there was an awkward moment.

We were standing there, facing each other. I was holding my nightgown and Minnie was holding the jogging suit.

"Oh well, what the hell," she said suddenly.

She took off her sneakers, her jeans, and her blouse. I took off my shoes, my slacks, and my cardigan sweater. We were nervously poised in our soggy underwear, staring at each other.

"Oh well, what the hell," I said.

I took off my bra and my panties. She did, too.

My mind flashed.

I saw Francine LaMonica.

This was only the second time in my entire life when I was in the presence of totally naked woman.

There was something in the air of my bedroom just then, something which didn't belong, something strange, something which I felt I needed to avoid, and yet at the same time, something which I desperately wanted to approach. Then I remembered my earliest memory, being mesmerized by the ocean, frightened yet intrigued by a carousel of stimuli which had beckoned me to come closer.

Ursula, come closer. Closer.

I took a step toward her, embraced her, feeling her bare chest gently press into mine, her arms slowly being brought around my shoulders, her stomach pushing into mine.

We kissed each other, slowly at first, our lips meeting with the lightest of contact, gently, warm, moist, then with a slightly harder pressure, then with passion.

We went to the bed.

We lay down in each other's arms.

Time seemed to slow, the seconds to minutes, the minutes to hours.

I gave myself to her.

She gave herself to me.

It was enchanting.

I thought of David.

I fantasized he was sitting in the chair near the bed, watching us, staring at us, his passions rising as fast as ours.

In my ears I heard his voice, the melodious sounds of French words. He was coaching us, directing us, his hands and arms pointing and flailing, telling us what to do to each other.

All of his words were in a language I didn't understand.

21

Wednesday, January 3, 2001
Hoyt Street

Vanessa woke to several strong knocks at her door.

She reluctantly got out of bed. She was still wearing her street clothes from yesterday. Her backpack lay unpacked at the foot of her bed.

She let Brenda in. They went into the kitchen. Vanessa made some coffee.

"You okay, Van?" Brenda asked.

"Yes, Bren," she moped, "I'm fine, I'm fine."

They sat next to one another on stools before the kitchen island. They waited for the coffee to perk.

Brenda wondered aloud, "Then what you doing here now?"

Brenda was looking at her. Vanessa was leaning her chin into the palms of her hands, her elbows seemingly impaled into the counter like fenceposts.

Then Brenda said, "I thought you said you didn't know when you were coming back here. I thought you said you were going to stay with Jeremy and like help out, cook him meals, run errands for him, things like that."

She had wasted little time with Vanessa.

If anything, Brenda was very perceptive, smart in the way of discerning from people's looks, their voice intonations, their subtle eye movements and body language, exactly how they were feeling, almost exactly what they were thinking.

At this moment, Brenda could smell trouble and taste disappointment. She sensed hurt and devastation, too. Lots of it.

"Look, Bren," Vanessa said, "I'm tired and I need to go back to bed so help yourself to the coffee."

"No, babydoll," Brenda said with determination in her voice, "you're going to tell me what happened."

Vanessa started crying.

The coffee was ready. Brenda got up, snatched two mugs and some sugar packets from a tumbler inside the cabinet above the sink, milk from the refrigerator, then slid her stool closer to Vanessa's and sat down.

Vanessa composed herself enough to tell Brenda what had happened, how she couldn't get to see Jeremy when she arrived at the hospital Monday night, how she had camped out and overslept in the lobby, and then how she finally had seen him in his room the next morning, grieving with his mother-in-law.

"I drove Jeremy from the hospital to his house in the Bronx, and the whole time neither of us spoke along the way. It was weird. When we got there, he got out of the car, and I did, too, and then I followed him up the walk to the door of his house. Brenda, he was shaking, like this," she waved her hands rapidly as if bolts of electricity were going through them, "fumbling for like five minutes trying to get the damn key into the lock, and then when he did, he opened the door for me to go inside. And then he saw my backpack for the first time. He looked at me," she stopped to stare at Brenda, a cold sheet of ice suddenly coming down in front of her eyes, "he looked at me, Bren, I mean if looks could kill, like I was nothing."

Brenda asked, "What do you mean?"

Vanessa cleared her throat. "I mean I went inside and I saw this big old trunk he has there against the wall in the living room, and on top are maybe a dozen little picture frames, and I'm looking at photographs of his wife, and pictures of his son, and shots of them together, and, well, I felt like I was, well you know, like I was—"

Brenda interrupted her. "Like you were trespassing, an intruder, like you didn't belong there?"

"Yes, yes," Vanessa said, "yes, like I'm violating some sacred ground or something. Then I'm thinking, What am I doing here? I mean, I just wanted to help him, not to intrude or to get in the way or anything, and then I realized that my being there with him was a really bad idea, a really, really bad idea."

Brenda held Vanessa's hands in hers. "Babydoll, you're a sweet girl, you like helping people. Look at what you do for a living. You try to help people all the time. You're sensitive and caring, sometimes too much, and besides, you care about Jeremy, you're his coworker, and you're his friend."

"Yes, but I felt like his whore then, Bren."

They were silent for a few minutes.

Then Vanessa poured more coffee for both of them.

"So?" Brenda asked. "It doesn't matter what you were thinking or how you felt, only that you were there to help him."

"Help him?" Vanessa shouted.

She took a moment to calm herself. "Bren, all of a sudden he's looking at me like I'm his bitch, his dirty street whore who cheated with him on his wife, his skinny little slut who's invading his space now. Everything changed then, everything. He was so angry to me. I felt his anger, I felt his rage. It was strangling me to death."

Brenda put her left arm around Vanessa's shoulders, raking the fingers of her right hand through Vanessa's long curls, trying to console her.

"Babydoll, it was just guilt. His wife's dead. You've slept with him. It caught up to him, and to you, too, right then and there. You weren't welcome there anymore."

Vanessa pleaded, "All I wanted to do was to help him, maybe cook some meals for him, help him with the little things, go to the store for him, whatever."

"What did he say? Anything?" Brenda asked.

"He didn't have to say anything, Bren. He just stood there, staring at me, his anger and his guilt punching at me, stabbing at me, suffocating me."

Vanessa got up and went to the window. She stared down at the small backyard, the abandoned swimming pool, then off into the distance past the limits of the property.

Brenda went to her.

"Van, Van, my baby," Brenda cooed.

They hugged. They kissed each other's lips.

Then Brenda asked, "How did he leave it with you?"

"I was devastated."

Vanessa slid her fingers across her cheeks to wipe away her tears.

"He whispered, 'Get out, please get out.'"

22

January 1, 1979
Manhattan

$\mathcal{N}$ew Year's Day.

The end of something, the beginning of something.

Transition.

Although I grew up in Nassau County on Long Island, just a stone's throw from New York City, well, maybe a long stone's throw, I really never considered myself metropolitan. By the time I was eighteen, I had been in and out of the city many times, yet every time I would go there it always seemed to me to be rather like a foreign country, one which didn't require a passport, but one which was very, very different from the sleepy suburbia I knew, the slower, less crowded, less diverse world which I was used to in Hicksville.

Someone once had said that architecture is frozen music, and since my eyesight was always 20/20, I think it's even a little better than that, I often would compare and contrast my favorite landmark, the magnificent Chrysler Building, which I had visited a hundred times, to the basic little cape in the middle of the woods some thirty or forty miles away that was my home from the time I was six or seven until the time I went off to college. Surely, a universe apart.

And since my hearing was always so acute, I often would weigh the sounds from the thousand grids of noisy city thoroughfares with their countless cars and trucks and buses, teeming like aggravated termites swarming out of control throughout a nest, the vehicles' horns constantly blaring, their tires screeching, their drivers screaming and cursing, all of that against the eerily quiet side street where I had lived, just off Newbridge Road, appropriately named Flower Street, the only real disturbance ever being Mr. LaMonica's blue Buick, constantly in need of a new muffler, on its clamorous way to and from Francine's house on Monroe Street, just around the corner and down a few blocks.

New York City. The five boroughs.

I remember years and years ago when I was fifteen, maybe sixteen, my boyfriend at the time, Keith Leach, and I had taken a smelly bus into Brooklyn to see Alan Freed's Rock'n'Roll Show at the Paramount Theater. It was simple, basic. But it was magic, too, so exciting and so much fun, even when compared to today's concerts with their kaleidoscopic light shows and spare-no-expense technology which often make them seem like other-worldly, hallucinogenic dreams, and sometimes nightmares, of glaring lights and blaring sounds, all come to life like Frankenstein's monster birthed from the dead.

Keith and I were mesmerized then, watching and listening to Little Anthony and The Imperials, Ral Donner, The Drifters, Jerry Lee Lewis, Little Richard, Martha and The VanDellas, and, of course, the headliners, The Ronettes. Until the time came for Ronnie Spector to strut her stuff, everyone waited intently. The audience became silent and still, like medical students in a gallery witnessing a master surgeon during a delicate operation. I still see her in my mind, and I still hear her booming voice in my ears, the exact moment when she pranced on stage and started singing "Be My Baby."

Anyway, in June of last year, lost again in my reveries of when I had been in New York City, I decided I'd visit again. I had made arrangements with a car service from Newburgh, Visconti Limousines, to take me from my home on Schreiber's Lane to the city, through and around the Bohemian hot spots, the

Village and SoHo, and also to Chinatown, Central Park, Columbus Circle, Rockefeller Center, Times Square, and, of course, my favorite, at 42nd Street and Lexington Avenue, the Chrysler Building.

I just had wanted to see and to hear the city again. And maybe I'd do some shopping, too.

When we were nearing Columbus Circle, I told the driver to stop at the Brill Building. I wanted to drop in on an old, well, I guess I can use the words now, an old friend.

I was in Bill Kaufman's office on the twelfth floor, explaining to the woman at the reception desk that, No, I didn't have an appointment, and, Yes, I was sure Mr. Kaufman would see me in a heartbeat.

He did.

We talked for a while, his pear-shaped housefly on his chin a little farther away from his mouth now, the result of time and aging, and sagging skin. He was very cordial to me. I had expected him to be. Years ago, he had come to me to make me a rich woman, and in the process, he had become rich, too. So, I guess we had some sort of symbiotic relationship all these years, distant yet intimate, but only in the financial sense of course, because every time I cashed a royalty check and a residual check, he did, too.

I didn't stay long then, but when I did leave his office I was very content and pleased with the new arrangement we had made. Mr. Kaufman had his own side business as the owner of a company which made audio tapes of famous and not-famous people reading their own or others' works. It was called BestSellers Cassettes.

"Your voice was always distinct to me," he had told me, "I think a tad lower and breathier than most women's voices, but also clear, and you enunciate well, getting the most out of your b's, d's, p's, t's, and m's,"

"Thank you, Bill. I'm E-flat, usually. You're in the majority, key of F."

"What?" he asked.

"Never mind," I said.

So, I would be coming into the city to the Brill Building every few months or so, reading a text aloud, my voice recorded on tape, the finished product intended for those people who could not read, found it difficult doing so, didn't want to, or for those who were blind, or for those who preferred just to listen to literature rather than to music, news, sports, or commentary from the radio, or to watch something droll on television. I had volunteered, telling Mr. Kaufman I didn't expect to be paid directly, but that I wanted the money, my modest fee for doing it and the small residual I insisted on for each tape which was sold, to be sent to the David Henry Writers Fund at the State University College at New Paltz, a grant program I had established in David's memory a few years ago.

The Fund provides three months' salary for public middle and high school teachers of English. The grants are supplemental, a stipend of sorts, allowing the teachers to take the three months off during the summer months to pursue their Master's degrees in English or to work on their writing, so they don't have to torture themselves teaching summer school, which David frequently had told me was little more than crowd control, or to have to take other jobs to augment their regular salaries. The Writers Fund was one of the ways I wanted to give something back, to keep myself busy, and another way for me to preserve my memories of David.

I had started the BestSellers Cassettes thing with Mr. Kaufman the second week in January, almost exactly a year ago, and even though my first recording took nine long days, Dee Brown's *Bury My Heart at Wounded Knee*, it was fun.

Then, after five or six more times during the subsequent months, the long rides to the city and the stay-overs at hotels had started to get to me.

So, I went apartment hunting.

Originally, I had thought that would do. But then, the real estate agent I was dealing with suggested I buy a house. My first reactions were, In the city? Move? Sell my house in New Paltz? Our house, David's and mine?

I would never do that.

And then I realized I had come to enjoy more and more the hustle and bustle of the city, its vibrancy, its opportunities, and its liveliness I perceived when I was there. But I knew in my heart of hearts I could never sell our farmhouse. I could never let go of my David that way.

Then it came to pass.

I decided I would buy a place in the city, stay there for a few weeks every other month or so to get the tapes done, and still keep our house in New Paltz as my primary residence.

I bought a row of three abutting vacant brownstones on East 57th Street and had them renovated. They were like bookends with one book in the middle. The ones on the ends each had three two-bedroom apartments, and the one in the middle I kept whole, for myself. Now, I was a New York City resident, at least for several weeks of the year, and a landlord, too.

I felt I remained true to David and to my memories of him. I still was attached to him professionally, in the sense that I often was in the place where the switch had been turned on at the LoneStar Literary Agency, and then later at Paramount Pictures.

And in the personal and intimate sense, I still had our home in New Paltz, that special place which had brought me so much pleasure and so much pain.

23

Thursday, January 4, 2001
Manhattan

Vanessa's shift was busy, but not too eventful. There were three false alarms, in addition to an abandoned car set on fire in a vacant lot, an electrical disturbance of some sort which had caused a small fire in the basement of a cafe, and a rash of dumpster fires, probably ignited by homeless people to create warmth, or maybe by morons having what they thought was some leftover fun from New Year's Eve.

Jeremy Myers was absent, still mourning the loss of his wife and child. The funeral services were scheduled for tomorrow, Friday.

There remained solemnity everywhere at the firehouse, on the firefighters' faces, in their low murmured voices when they spoke, and in the air. Vanessa had helped to hang purple bunting from each of the second-floor locker room windows which faced out to the street. Grief was everywhere.

At 10:15 p.m., Vanessa's unit returned to the firehouse from the car fire. Most of the crew huddled near the long table on the side of one of the engine bays, drinking coffee, eating donuts, chatting about football, the unusually severe cold snap which had been gripping the city for the past few days, anything to derail their thoughts about Jeremy.

Vanessa went to the snack room.

The large room had several vending machines filled with cans of soda, juices and iced tea, cheap pastries, small packages of cookies, chips, pretzels, candy bars, cigarettes, coffee, hot chocolate, and, of all things, three different kinds of condoms. Some of the firemen still held to the old saws that there's just something about a man in uniform, and to always be prepared.

Men.

At one end of the room, there were six metal folding chairs and a rectangular table braced against the side of a stairwell which led upstairs to the locker rooms, supply cabinets, rest rooms, and the briefing room.

In the snack room, the light bulb in the old ceiling fixture had blown out over a week ago, but no one had bothered to replace it. There were only faint glows from the vending machines and a shaft of dim light coming down the stairwell from the lighted hallway upstairs.

Vanessa got herself a diet Pepsi, then sat down on one of the chairs, leaning her forearms on the table, holding the soda can in her hands, staring at its logo. She was lost in thought about Jeremy, what he must be going through now, and the awkward moments at his house two days ago where there was so much guilt, sorrow, anger and rage.

Lieutenant Tony Vly and Captain Tom Angola came into the snack room.

"Hey, Nessa," Tom said.

Tony asked, "What's up, Van?"

She didn't look up.

Tony huffed at her, then said, "Look, Van, it's terrible what happened, but life goes on. He'll regroup and he'll recover. That's something we all should do. What are we supposed to do, moan and mope all day long from now to Memorial Day? Let this teach you a lesson. Shit happens."

Then, as Tony fumbled with some change in front of one of the vending machines, "Maybe it's time for the three of us to get our minds off things."

Vanessa shuddered at Tony's cold words. She sensed

something, something in the way he said 'get our minds off things,' something in his thoughtless dismissal of what had happened coupled with his obvious lack of genuine compassion.

She got up, turning to look at Tony and Tom.

"What's that supposed to mean?" she asked both of them.

Tom was silent.

From over his shoulder, Tony said, "Hey, baby, easy now, you just need to relax, you need to have some fun."

"Have some fun?" she asked.

"Yes, some fun," Tony said, craning his neck to look into her eyes. "We'll all be out of here in about an hour and a half or so, then you, me and Tom, you know what I'm saying, we—"

"No, I don't know what you're saying, Tony," she snapped, "so why don't you just break it down for me?"

She was being sarcastic and belligerent to him, and Tony didn't like it.

He turned his body to confront her. His tone changed.

"Look, bitch," he whispered, pointing his finger at her, "when we're outta here you go right home and then me and Tom'll meet you there. You get all dolled up for us, you understand?"

Vanessa turned around to the table, reaching for the soda can. She picked it up, turned back to face them, and then stared at Tony. There was anger in her eyes, her mind was reeling with disbelief, her stomach knotting from rage. She was strangling the can with her hand.

"And then what?" she screamed at both of them.

Tom said, "Hey, take it easy, Nessa, it's just we thought—"

"Then what?" she screamed at Tony, "then you and him going to do me again? Beat me? Screw me? Use me like a whore?"

Tom hurriedly left the snack room.

"Well?" Vanessa yelled.

Tony pulled a spring-loaded lever and a candy bar crashed into the machine's cradle. "You stupid cunt," Tony said, approaching her head on. He grabbed her elbows in his hands, pushing her backward a few steps, shaking her. "Don't you ever raise your voice to me, you understand me? What the hell's the matter now? All of a sudden you got a problem with what I do to you?"

He stopped shaking her.

She was still in his grasp.

She looked up into his eyes.

They were windows, and Vanessa didn't like anymore what she saw inside Tony. Then, they were mirrors, and she realized she couldn't stand to look at the reflection of herself.

She freed her arms from him, retreating a few steps, her eyes wide, her blood boiling in her veins, her mind spinning.

She took a deep breath, composing herself.

She said slowly, "I never had a problem with what you do to me Tony, only now with what you are. If you ever come on to me again, I'll drop by and tell all our hot little stories to your wife, and then I'll get some hungry lawyer to chase you down and nail your sorry ass to the wall for all that locker room business, you understand?"

He looked at her, said nothing, then left the room.

Vanessa collapsed in the chair.

She was exhausted.

Yet, she finally felt release, not only the letting go of her emotions, but also the cleansing freedom now to begin to go on with her life without Tony dominating her.

It was the first time in her life she ever had stood up to a man.

24

August 1982
Schreiber's Lane

$\mathcal{M}$y home is approximately three miles south outside the village of New Paltz. After a left turn off Route 32, which continues on through the hamlet of Modena to the city of Newburgh, my front door is about three hundred yards down Schreiber's Lane.

The house was built in 1937. It has three stories, a sort of a Victorian-style design, originally a home for a farming family from Scandinavia, Olsen, I think was their name, set on about two acres. When David bought it in 1967, it was bordered on its left side by a small expanse of woods and some marsh, acres of apple orchards stretching from the limits of the backyard farther eastward, and flat, heavily wooded land on its right. The topography hasn't changed much since then, except the orchards out back no longer are worked and the marsh has swelled some, almost to a well-defined stream.

About twelve years ago, a local developer from Maybrook, James Palen, bought ten acres which front both Route 32 and Schreiber's Lane, put in a road, Palentine Place, and then built eleven modest raised-ranch homes. They were far enough away from our house so as not to seem like they were encroaching in any way, but close enough so that David and I could look out our second-story bedroom window and see the backyards of several of the houses.

David loved spying on our neighbors sometimes.

I had come to enjoy New York City so much that I had decided to live in my brownstone on East 57th Street for what roughly corresponded to the school year, from Labor Day until Memorial Day. I liked being there in the thick of things, especially during November, December, January and February, and even March sometimes, when the troublesome weather, the ice, sleet and snow, didn't seem to be as much of a problem for the New York City Department of Sanitation there as it was for the New Paltz Highway Department here upstate. I had tired of fighting the cold in the Hudson Valley by myself, and I had grown accustomed to the city's hustle and bustle, the lights, the music of motion on the streets and in the air, and the vibrancy of city life which, I felt, counteracted the doldrums and the winter's often relentless discontent.

I decided I would rent our house on Schreiber's Lane during the cold weather when I was in the city because I didn't want it to be empty for that long of a period of time. I wanted someone to be there to see that the pipes didn't freeze, and in my heart of hearts, and in what I guess is an odd way, I wanted someone to share what David and I had shared.

I would return to New Paltz for the summer months, from Memorial Day until Labor Day, when the fresh air, clear blue skies and warm weather returned to me serene memories of sense and feeling, not only because it had been in August when my voyage with David had begun, but also because I had aged. Now, at thirty-six, I was finding more and more that I was increasingly sensitive to the cold. My skinny body hated what seemed to be a more severe and penetrating raw coldness slinking through the unencumbered air of the country. It just didn't seem as bad in the concrete canyons of New York City.

Yesterday, I took a leisurely walk on Schreiber's Lane toward Palen's development and Route 32. I knew of a large stand of day lilies which grew defiantly by the edge of the road along the way, and I wanted to snip some and put them in a vase on my kitchen table.

I was busy snipping when I heard children's voices.

I turned to see two young girls walking hand-in-hand on the side of the road talking to each other, slowly coming toward me— they hadn't seen me yet—dressed in identical outfits, scarlet-colored blouses, blue denim bib overalls and white sneakers. They were sisters, I could tell. One looked about 9, the other maybe 6 or 7. Each had a bright red ribbon tied to her hair at the top of her head. I knew they couldn't be, but they looked almost like twins, both with dark curly hair, bright eyes, clean skin, dark brows and pleasant faces. They were so adorable, but careless. They were walking now in the middle of the road, not realizing where they were. I had seen cars fly down this way many times, so I called out to them from the shoulder where I was snipping my lilies.

"Girls, girls, look where you are," I said, nodding my head to the middle of the road, "you need to be careful here, okay?"

They looked at me.

I had startled them. They were frightened.

The older girl immediately understood what I had meant about the road, now quickly walking toward the shoulder and toward me, her younger sister in tow.

"I'm sorry," I said, "I didn't mean to scare you. Hi, my name is Ursula and I live right over there," I said, pointing to my house.

They seemed at ease now even though I think they both had come to realize what they had been doing, perhaps in the backs of their minds now hearing the voice of their father or their mother admonishing them to 'Always stay out of the road.'

The older girl looked up at me and said, "Thank you."

"Sure," I said, "but tell me, where were you going? There's not too much down this way, you know. Wait, what are your names?"

The younger girl shyly whispered, "Lisa."

"Well," I said, "nice to meet you, Lisa."

She giggled. "No, not Lisa, Resa," she said to me, accenting the R.

"Oh my, I'm sorry, R-r-resa," I said, "what a beautiful name!"

"Thank you, Ursula," she said, "and this is my sis, Cynthia."

Cynthia smiled at me, and when she did her entire face lit up.

"And howdy doody to you, too, Cynthia," I said.

"Thank you, Ursula."

They both snickered.

The two of them, I thought, smart, cute, and polite, too.

"Now, where were you guys going?" I asked.

Resa said, "Well, today's my daddy's birthday and when he comes home later we were thinking about what we should do for him."

"Here? On the road?" I asked.

Cynthia said, "No, I mean it's our talk place so mommy doesn't hear. She said she'd take us shopping in a little while, but we want to do something for her, too."

I wanted both of them in my house right now, sitting on my cozy couch in their jammies, nice and snug, eating strawberries and cream, my reading a silly story to them, listening to them giggling, watching them drinking big glasses of chocolate milk.

"Oh, okay," I said. "Any ideas?"

"Not really," Resa said sadly.

"Well," I reasoned, "any minute now your mom is going to start worrying because she doesn't know where you guys are right now. So, you walk back home, on the shoulder," I emphasized, "and I'll go back to my house and see if I can think of something. Then I'll drive by your house and let you know what I came up with, okay?"

"Sure," they said together, turning their heads to one another.

"Okay, Cynthia and Resa, you go home now, on the shoulder, and then sit in front of your house and wait for me. Maybe ten minutes. You got it?"

In unison they said, "Got it!"

"Good!" I said.

As they walked back holding hands, I remained there by the lilies to observe, just in case they would wander too far into the road. They didn't. I saw them arrive safely at the second house on Palentine. I ran home to figure out what I could do for them.

Later, I drove over to their house. They were sitting on the bottom step of their front stoop, still holding hands. I wanted to kiss them to death. When I pulled up, they rushed toward me. I saw their mother at the window, watching. I waved to her. She waved back.

"Hi, guys," I said, as they leaned in the passenger side window. "Is it okay for you to be with me?"

"Yes," Cynthia said, "we told mommy all about you and where you live, but we left out the part about being in the middle of the road."

"Your secret is safe with me," I said, holding up my right hand, two fingers crossed.

They smiled at me. I could see genuine relief in their eyes.

Smart. Polite. Just two good kids, I thought.

"Hey, I have something for you," I teased.

A duet from them. "What? What? What is it? Tell me. What is it? No, tell me! No, me!"

I had scoured my house for something to bring to them. I really didn't have any appropriate things so I had had to improvise.

"Here is something for your mommy," I said, handing Cynthia a Waterford crystal vase filled with a spray of bright-orange day lilies. "You just need to put some water in it later, okay?"

"Wow," she said, slowly feeling the cut crystal pattern with her long fingers, "this is beautiful."

"And for daddy on his birthday, this."

I handed Resa a wooden box, about the size of a large cigar box, one of two I had on my dresser in my bedroom. David had bought them years ago, before we were together, when he had vacationed with his wife in the West through New Mexico, Arizona, Utah and Colorado. They were a matching set, ceremonial boxes of some sort from the Navaho. Each had two small brass hinges and a brass hasp, and a tiny lock and key. Both were finely handmade from blonde almost white wood with intricate carvings on the lids. One carving pictured an old Navaho woman, dressed in a handmade ornamental cloak, standing quietly, meditatively, surrounded by an embracing cove of boulders, peering at her reflection in the still pool of water at her feet, lost, perhaps, in prayer or reminiscences, maybe seeking out her god or daydreaming memories of her past. The other, which I handed to Resa now, showed a Navaho warrior on horseback, his magnificent stallion rearing, the warrior's long hair, his headdress, his spear feathers and the horse's mane straining in the wind, the man and his charge consumed with the anticipation of battle.

"Wow," Resa said, with the identical breathy tone and slow inflection her sister had used just moments ago, "wow."

"Open it," I said.

Inside was the key to the lock, and a silver bracelet David had bought when he was at the reservation. It was a box chain with quarter-inch rectangular links and a strong clasp with a small turquoise stone set into it, an understated but very masculine and tasteful piece of Navaho jewelry.

"Wow," Resa said again.

"Okay, guys, now you run inside and try to hide these behind your backs and tell your mommy her new neighbor from down there on Schreiber's would like her to accept these secret things as, well, let's just say it's the neighborly thing to do, okay? And see if you can find some tissue paper and some wrapping paper for these gifts. Got it?"

They were so happy and excited that they thoughtlessly ran in front of my car into the middle of Palentine Place coming around to my window, standing on tiptoes, pushing their heads and upper torsos into the car to offer me kisses.

"Thank you, Ursula, thank you, thank you, thank you, thank you," they chirped.

I kissed them both, then told them to get going.

They ran from me, carefully carrying their bounty behind them, across their lawn, up the stairs, and into their house.

I drove away, so pleased with them and with myself that I then decided I would just motor along the sleepy country roads for a while to enjoy the freedom of this glorious summer day.

I hadn't driven long when I realized I was crying.

I was regretting, again, that I never was able to deliver David a child.

25

Friday, January 5, 2001
Manhattan

At the firehouse, Vanessa Fernandez was on her way up the stairs to the locker room. When she got there, she noticed the door.

It wasn't slanting anymore. It wasn't ajar.

She entered the locker room, then carefully closed the door behind her, hearing its bolt sliding easily into the strike plate. She tried pulling on the knob. The door was secure.

Someone had fixed the bottom hinge.

She went to her locker, opened it, and saw inside the delicate gold chain and heart pendant hanging from the coat hook.

She held the pendant in her fingertips.

Something for me always to come back to, she thought.

"Hi, Van."

Vanessa turned to see Donna Lewis. Donna was the company's clerk on the shift, an all-around assistant to Fire Captain Tom Angola and to Lieutenant Tony Vly, a secretary, desk monitor, phone jockey, memorandum-maker, and chief cook and bottle washer of sorts. She was fifty-seven years old, with medium-length, striking red hair knotted in tight curls, but not knotted quite tightly enough to hide a few sheaves of equally striking black roots sprouting at the crown of her head. She had prominent cheekbones and a small scar near her upper lip. Her face was weathered, partly from age, and partly from a lonely life since the passing of her husband more than a decade ago. Her eyes, though deep-set, still sparkled. Her teeth were small, her mouth thin.

It was 3:51 p.m. Donna had come upstairs to grab a sweater from her locker, a few spaces down from Vanessa's.

"Oh, hi, Donna," Vanessa said. "I'm sorry, I was thinking of somewhere else. How you doing?"

"Not good, Van. A few of us went to the funerals this morning. It was so sad."

Vanessa exhaled. "I just couldn't bring myself to go, Donna. I hope Jeremy understands. It's just I can't handle those things. I bought some carnations on my way in and just before I came up here I put them on the table in the snack room, just to, well, I guess just to do something, a little memorial of sorts I guess."

"It's okay, Van. We each grieve in our own way."

Donna liked Vanessa. When Vanessa was hired, Donna understood right away what certainly lay ahead of her in this place, the looks, the sexual comments under breaths, the leers, the come-ons. Donna had done her best to quell what could be quelled by watching out for Vanessa, monitoring her in a motherly way when the guys were in her presence, quickly and sternly warning them to tread lightly or to back off when she thought they were creeping nearer to the line that shouldn't be crossed.

"Anyway, let me make your day," Donna said, smiling.

"What?" Vanessa asked, staring into Donna's eyes.

Donna handed Vanessa a business card. She took it.

"What's this?" Vanessa wondered.

"Geez, Van, a test and you forgot to study. Hello, it's a business card. Read it."

Vanessa read aloud, "Jacobs, Weires, Russert and Partners, Attorneys at Law, The Manchester Building, 12 Wall Street, New York, New York."

"No, silly," Donna kidded, "the back. Read the note on the back."

She turned the card over in her hand. She read, "I'm in

heaven. Where's my angel? 845-255-1873."

Vanessa beamed.

"Donna, where did you get this?"

"Here. Downstairs. Tom had asked me to come in an hour early today, you know how I need the overtime, and so I did, and then about ten after three, this tall, handsome buck strolls in looking for Vanessa Fernandez, so I told him you'd been transferred to Oregon and that I'd be glad to—"

"Donna!" Vanessa blurted, "you didn't. I mean you didn't say—"

"No, no, honey," Donna said with some giggles in her breath, "no, I'm kidding. I told him you weren't in yet, that my name was Donna, but he could call me Darling, and I asked him if he'd like to wait a bit for you."

"And?" Vanessa asked impatiently.

"And then he said he really wanted to but that he had to get to Grand Central to catch a train upstate. He asked me to give you his card. Of course, I made a photo copy of it for myself."

Vanessa laughed. "Thanks, Donna. But don't you think he's a little too, well you know, a little—"

"What," Donna barked, "a little what? Listen, honey, I may be rusty," she ran her hands through her red hair, "but I haven't forgotten how to lie down on my back or how to eat a banana!"

They laughed for a few moments. Then, they realized it was almost four o'clock, time to get to the briefing room. Donna returned to her locker, got her sweater, closed the locker, then went downstairs. Vanessa changed her top and then placed the business card on the locker shelf.

"Something for me always to come back to," she said aloud.

At the briefing, Captain Tom Angola addressed the unit with a short, though well-spoken homily regarding the tragedy which had befallen one of their own, Jeremy Myers, and then called for a moment of silence. Thoughtfully, he had begun each briefing this way since New Year's Day.

Next was some information regarding personnel scheduling for an imminent manpower shortage at a neighboring firehouse which, if it developed, would require most of this group to work double shifts. Everyone moaned.

Vanessa was off, daydreaming. Then, she looked at Tony Vly. He was standing next to Tom.

He looked back at her.

Vanessa felt a sudden chill, the ice from his eyes burning into hers. Indeed, his eyes had changed. They were so different now. His cold look was sinister and filled with anger, not with the sensuous mix of passion and frustration which she had seen in it the many times when he had wanted to use her. She could tell that he knew he no longer could control her when he wanted to, and that she no longer wanted him to. His ego had been shattered by the will of a woman. He was seething with anger.

Vanessa looked away.

I'll take my chances, she thought.

When the shift was over, Vanessa left the firehouse and decided to stop at Fiore's Bar for a little while rather than to go home to her apartment in Brooklyn. Even though she was tired, she knew she wouldn't be able to sleep right away.

The look in Tony's eyes still haunted her.

No sense rushing home to a nightmare, she thought.

She walked into Fiore's to her usual chorus of welcome. She threw her jacket to Fiore, then slid a bar stool next to her bald friend, Douglas, who was sucking from a straw impaled in his beer bottle.

"Hi, Douglas," Vanessa said, settling herself. Then, "Don't you have a home to go to? Why are you always here when I'm here?"

He smiled at her. "Yeah, baby, I do, but it's lonesome there. Here I have lots of company. You know, my Irish friends, Mr. Bud Weiser, Mr. Jack Daniels and Mr. Johnny Walker. The Spanish mafia, too, Señor Heiniken, Señor Miller, Señor Corona, in sublime addition to all those tasty ales old man Fiore keeps on tap. Oh, and don't forget the love of my life, Señorita Martini. How 'bout you, sweetie? If I'm always here when you're here, then you're always here when I'm—"

"Okay, okay," Vanessa said good-naturedly, leaning over to kiss Douglas on his cheek, "you win, you win."

"You're a doll, Van," he said, blushing from her kiss.

Suddenly, Vanessa felt someone at her back, gently pushing into her, kissing the crown of her head.

She quickly turned around.

"Jimmy!" she said with genuine surprise in her voice, "Jimmy, Jimmy! I thought you went back to wherever it was, I thought you had a train to catch."

He was standing there, holding a glass of Colombard in one hand, and a glass of seltzer with lemon, no ice, in the other.

"I missed it," he said, handing her the glasses, "and I missed you."

"How sweet," she said, taking the drinks from him, "you remembered. Thank you, Jimmy."

Vanessa reached over to drag an unoccupied bar stool closer to her. Jimmy sat down.

They chatted for a while. Vanessa found herself gradually becoming fonder of Jimmy, the way he spoke, with the hint of a drawl every now and then, the constant vibrancy and animation in his voice, his hands and his body, and his big brown eyes which still reminded her of pools of sweet chocolate. From the moment she brazenly had introduced herself to him on New Year's Eve, Vanessa liked the way he spoke, his mannerisms, but what was even more intriguing to her now was the way he was listening to her. He seemed to strain to hear every word she said, as if he were processing each one, both for its definition in context as well as for its subtleties and shades of meaning. She could tell he was fascinated by the sounds of her words, too, as if her mix of hard English consonants and soft Spanish vowels was a code of some sort. She sensed it was a code he desperately wanted to break.

I like you a lot, Jimmy Russert, she thought.

Vanessa learned that James Russert was born in Kingston, New York, went to high school there, and then entered Boston University to do his undergraduate work, majoring in Criminal

Justice with a minor in English Literature. Then he went on to New York University Law School, graduating cum laude with a degree in corporate law. He worked for a small firm in uptown Manhattan for nine years, then accepted a position at a larger firm downtown in the financial district.

"I found myself on the fast track," he was telling her, "and after winning several well-publicized cases, I made partner three years later."

Vanessa did the math in her head.

He's probably around forty, she thought.

"You're forty, right?" she asked him.

"Good guess. Forty-two," he said. "And you're what? Twenty-five?"

"Maybe," she said, sipping the Colombard.

"Well," he said, "the French have a saying, that a man should be with a woman who's half his age plus seven."

Almost perfect, she mused to herself.

Then, aloud, "I'll be twenty-seven in August."

Fiore came over. "Another round, Nessa?"

"Yes, please," she said to him, "and a bourbon for my friend here."

"How sweet," Jimmy said, "you remembered."

Vanessa kissed him on the cheek.

"So, where do you live?" she asked.

"Depends on what month it is," Jimmy answered.

"No, really," she insisted, "where are the wife and kids?"

He bristled.

"Hey, I'm not like that," he said. "I'm not married, never have been."

"Okay, okay," she said, "I'm sorry. I'm sorry, Jimmy. It's just there always seems to be, well, you know, another woman in the picture already when I meet someone like you."

"Someone like me?" he asked.

"Yes, Jimmy Russert, someone like you."

Vanessa leaned into him, pressing her chest against his, kissing him gently on the lips. Then she slowly parted her lips from his, keeping her mouth close, whispering in a staccato rhythm, "Now, tell me where you live."

His whispered back, his breath brushing against her lips, "What month is this?"

She reared back from him, laughing.

He took a sip of bourbon. "Vanessa, I'm teasing you. I have a townhouse in New Jersey and I'm there most of the time, but I like to ski. A lot. I grew up in and around the shadows of Hunter Mountain upstate, so for the winters I usually rent a place near there to be close to the slopes."

"I see," Vanessa said. "I've never skied. Want to teach me sometime?"

"Well, that's why I'm here tonight."

"Just to teach me to ski?" she asked, with a breathy coyness in her voice.

Old habits die hard.

"No, no," he said. He sipped his bourbon again, then placed the glass on the bar. His forearms rested there, his hands now cupping the glass. He was staring at the glass as he spoke to her.

"Vanessa, I'd like you to come upstate with me for a long weekend, if you can take a few days off, and stay at the house I'm renting. We can ski, hike, ice skate, sit around the fireplace, drink seltzer and lemon—"

"No ice," she said.

He smiled. "Right, no ice, or maybe we can munch on some fava beans and drink Chianti. Oh, I didn't tell you my middle name is Hannibal?"

Vanessa laughed again.

She drank more of the Colombard.

"Jimmy," she said softly, "look at me."

He turned to her.

"I'd love to stay with you for a few days. Thanks for the invite. I'll make arrangements with Donna, my clerk, and I'll go with you, but," a slight hesitancy, "but, well, there've been some changes with me these last few days, Jimmy, and, well, I need to say something."

"What is it?" he asked.

She drew in her breath. "I'll go, but please understand I might want my own room."

Vanessa kept holding her breath, waiting. She wasn't sure what Jimmy's reaction would be.

He smiled.

"Absolutely," he said, "as you wish." Then, "Great, I'll make my arrangements then, too."

Vanessa felt a warm pillow of relief engulf her.

I like you a lot, Jimmy Russert, she thought.

They raised their glasses, brought them together, then sipped, then kissed. They could taste the magical blend of bitter bourbon and sweet Colombard from each other's lips.

She asked, "So where's the house? Like near Kingston?"

"No," he said, "it's a little place just outside the village of New Paltz."

26

August 1985
New Paltz

$\mathcal{A}$s I write this, I find myself nearing a perilous cusp.

Next year, I'll be forty years old.

I know it's been said that life begins at forty, but lately I've been wondering.

Maybe it ends there.

Anyway, it's been unusually warm and annoyingly humid here this summer, today being the twelfth consecutive day the temperature has been at or above ninety degrees. For more than a week and a half now, in and around the house I've worn only my panties and skimpy t-shirts, the kind with no sleeves, David's favorite outfit for me when we would swelter together here during the summers. David hated what he called the false atmosphere of air conditioning, so we never bothered with central air.

I've made countless pitchers of iced tea, and have drunk them all. At night, I've tossed and turned in bed from the lingering stuffiness and clammy stickiness which, paradoxically, seem so much more oppressive to me after the sun has set rather than before.

With my next birthday a milestone of sorts—or maybe it's a headstone, who knows?—I've decided I shall begin a personal inventory of sorts, to remember and to reminisce, to evaluate and to review, and to use what I have learned and what I have experienced as a guide as I prepare to seek out and to explore new avenues on which I will travel during the days and months to come.

Age, not space, is the final frontier.

Something has been troubling me for the past few days.

I've had my share of boys and men, and without meaning to sound fatuous, I think I've done it all. Let me try my hand at a really mundane metaphor. In junior high school my seed was planted, in high school it budded, in college it bloomed, and with my David, my insatiable David, it blossomed.

No wonder there's the word *deflowered*.

I understand what my role with men always has been, a role I willingly chose all along the way, and that was to surrender to them, to obey them, to offer myself to them in return for their attention, passion and love.

I am not embarrassed by this, nor do I feel any sense of disgust or degradation.

For me, it's always been a means to an end.

I've always known my place with men.

I know what I am.

And being that way, I've enjoyed so many of them, and hopefully they're enjoyed me.

But, it has gotten me to think.

I know I still believe that acts of physical intimacy, whatever they are for consenting adults, are what make the trials and tribulations of this everyday life bearable.

I still remember the Beatles' words: And in the end, all the love you take is equal to the love you make.

I know I still am tolerant of the many lifestyles people enjoy, and the words which may be used to describe their interactions: love, sex, prurience, worship, passion, homosexuality, adoration, aberrance, surrender, companionship, ardor, desire, lust.

Call it what you will, but in my heart of hearts I still believe each of us must call it often.

And yet, and this is what's been bothering me, looking back

now, I'm experiencing some doubt about whether my way with men, the role I chose, was really the best way for me.

I know what I had with them, being the way I am.

But what did I miss?

What did I endure which didn't need to be endured?

How many men have been strangers to me because of my ways, ignoring me, passing me over for others, dismissing me outright because my submission was so distasteful and so repugnant to them?

If I had harbored less doubt about myself, felt less vulnerable, less weak, if I had chosen not to surrender, not to obey, not to offer myself with abandon, but to thrust and to parry, so to speak, done less giving and more taking during courtships and interludes, stood up for myself, yes, yes, stood up for myself, if I had been stronger, more demanding, more selective, then would my life have been different?

I know life is too short.

And I've been thinking.

Would I have met someone, a different kind of man, a man who was sensitive, a man who always would treat me with respect, a man who would understand and respond to my wants, my needs and my desires, a man who often would compromise with me, a man who—

No. Never mind. I mustn't think along those lines now.

It's just too late for me.

27

Saturday, January 6, 2001
Hoyt Street

Vanessa had today off, so she stayed in her pajamas since waking at noon. She had read a few chapters from Anne Rice's *Blood and Gold*, watched an old DVD Donna Lewis had loaned her, *The Sixth Day*, with big Arnold in the starring role, wrote an E-mail to her younger sister Stephanie, and now was in the kitchen preparing rice to make her favorite dish, arroz con pollo.

She looked out her windows and saw snow peppering the backyard, the large wet flakes sticking to the weeds this way and that, gradually draping them. The sky was dark gray, almost black. It looked cold outside.

She went to the phone and dialed.

"Hello?"

"Hey, monkey, it's me. Come down and I'll make you an early dinner. Wait, it's almost two. Maybe a late lunch?"

"Sure! Be right down."

A few moments later, Brenda Villanueva knocked.

Opening the door, Vanessa said, "Wow, that was fast!"

"I'm hungry! Ummm, smells good!" Brenda said.

They hugged, kissing each other on the lips.

They went into the kitchen.

Vanessa got a brick of muenster cheese and some seedless

red grapes, a handful of crackers, then poured two glasses of wine. They sat on stools at the kitchen island while the rice cooked.

"So," Brenda asked, "everything all ready for your big weekend with your lawyer friend, mister what's-his-name?"

"Jimmy, Jimmy Russert," Vanessa said. "We haven't firmed it up yet, and I guess I'm looking forward to," she raised her left arm pointing to the windows, "getting away from all this for a few days, the city, the job, the, well, just everything."

"I know. Good for you. He going to teach you to ski?"

"I hope so," Vanessa said, biting into a grape. "I'd like to try. Imagine, a city girl like me in the country for the first time! I don't think I've ever been past the GW Bridge, that's as far north as I've ever been."

Brenda wasted no time scanning Vanessa's face, her eyes, and watching her body language. She sensed a slight tension. Brenda knew Vanessa really wasn't worried about the skiing. "So what's the big deal? He did you on New Year's Eve, right? What's to think about?" she asked innocently.

"Bren—da!" Vanessa said, loudly accenting the first syllable and then whispering the second.

They giggled.

"So, what's to think about?" Brenda asked again.

Vanessa reached for her glass of wine from the counter. She sipped. She looked into Brenda's eyes. "Well, I told him there've been some changes in me and—"

"And what? You told him you didn't want to sleep with him again?"

"No, Bren, I just said that I might want my own room."

"You're kidding, right?" Brenda asked.

"No, I just said I might. I didn't say I had to have it."

"You are kidding, aren't you? You know he likes you and you know he likes to, shit, they all do," she huffed, "men, they're all alike, and you think he's not thinking about—"

"Bren, I like him so much. I know he wants to do me again. I do, too. But, I've been thinking about making some changes. Big changes. I've been thinking about finding a new job, I want to change the way men see me, and I want to be—"

Brenda jumped in. "Wow, you aren't kidding! You want some respect, right?" She started singing Aretha's anthem, "R—E—S—P—E—C—T, hey—"

"I'm serious, Bren."

"Okay, okay, I'm sorry. So, just play it by ear. Relax. Have a good time. See what happens."

The rice was ready. Vanessa prepared two plates. They ate, gabbing about little things. When they finished, they did the dishes together, then went into the living room and sat on the couch together.

"I know it's crazy, Bren," Vanessa said, "but it's just something I want to have as an option with him. I don't know, maybe, just maybe it's time for me to try to—"

"I understand, really I do," Brenda said, "there are times when you have to drive your car a different way, right?" Then, "Hey, I know! Let's pack for you, okay?"

"It's a little early for that, Bren, but okay, what the hell."

They went into the bedroom.

Brenda sat at the foot of the bed. Vanessa threw a carry-all on the pillows, then went to her closet.

Sliding the hangars along, Vanessa said, "I know I'll need to bring thermals and heavy socks and sweaters, but I don't have any real ski stuff, and I guess I'll need to bring some fancy things in case we go out to dinner."

Frustrated with her closet, Vanessa went to her dresser. She fumbled through the drawers. Finally, she tossed two pairs of thermal long johns, three pairs of woolen socks, five pairs of panties, five bras, some sweaters, and two pairs of jeans onto the bed. Brenda took the clothing, carefully folded them, and then put them into the carry-all.

Vanessa went back to the closet. She took out a cobalt blue, sequined dress with spaghetti straps and a gathered bodice, holding it up for Brenda to see. "Too fancy?" she asked.

"Try it on," Brenda said.

Vanessa took off her pajama bottoms, then the top. She only had panties on. Brenda watched as Vanessa stretched to raise the dress above her head, letting it slide down over her face, putting her arms up through the straps, struggling a bit to get it past her breasts, then adjusting it over her torso so it fit properly.

"Well?" Vanessa asked.

"Put heels on. Let's see the whole picture."

Vanessa put on a pair of stilettos, then turned around a few times, her hands on her hips.

"Too fancy, but killer, Van," Brenda said.

Vanessa went to the closet again. "What about this?" she asked, holding a woolen suit, a matching dark red mini skirt and cropped military-style jacket.

"Nice, Van."

Vanessa brought her arms through the straps of the dress and then slid it down until it was on the floor. She stepped out of it, picked it up, hung it on its hanger, then went to return it to the closet.

Brenda stared at her again, seeing her there, facing into the closet, just in her panties and her heels. She looked at Vanessa's naked back, her panties clinging to her butt like Saran wrap, then at her legs.

Vanessa turned back around to Brenda, then put on the jacket, buttoning it. Then she put on the skirt. "Well?" she asked. "This okay?"

"Perfect," Brenda said. "Mind if I try on that blue one you had before?"

"Sure, go ahead."

Near the head of the bed, Vanessa took off the suit and began folding it while Brenda snaked out of her sweater—she wasn't wearing a bra—took off her sneakers and socks, then her jeans, straightened her panties which had drooped some, then went to the closet to get the blue dress. She got it, then turned around to see Vanessa standing in front of her.

There was an awkward moment.

"Bren," Vanessa asked tentatively, "why do we always kiss

each other on the mouth?"

Brenda thought for a moment.

"I don't know, Van," she said slowly, "we've been best buds since what, the third grade? I guess I, I mean, I guess we—"

They stepped toward each other.

They embraced, their breasts touching, then compressing. Then, their lips met.

They kissed, gingerly.

"I guess I just want to," Brenda whispered.

"Me, too," Vanessa said.

28

June 1988
Yankee Stadium

$\mathcal{D}$avid died almost eighteen years ago.

I've kept myself busy managing the David Henry Writers Fund, auditing all the French courses offered during the summers at the State University College, as well as other courses here and there, renovating and redecorating our house on Schreiber's Lane, reading almost anything I can get my hands on, writing some poems and some short stories and publishing a few with limited success, trying my hand at the tediousness of quilting and needlepoint, renovating and redecorating my brownstone on East 57th Street in New York City, doing lots of volunteer work across town at St. Luke's Hospital on Tenth Avenue, occasionally vacationing in New England, California and Florida, staying in touch with and visiting a few old friends, especially my college roommate Hadee Shah, attending writing conferences, going to Broadway plays, enjoying concerts and lectures, and becoming more and more interested in professional baseball.

But only the Yankees, of course.

I remember one game at Yankee Stadium in particular.

I was seated behind home plate, about six or seven rows up, with a spectacular view of the playing field, its rich, green grass, its patches of silky dirt around the bases and at the pitcher's mound, the amazing architecture, the glorious panorama and the mystifying aura of what truly is the house that Ruth built.

By the fourth inning, though, I had had a terrible headache.

Looking through that protective screen, constantly focusing and refocusing, seeing the action on the field blurred sometimes by the black mesh, squinting to see in between the little boxes— why not use that stuff they call plexiglass, maybe with some small air holes drilled through it?—all had made my temples throb. And, not to help matters any, an insufferably annoying man was next to me, continuously yelling and screaming, constantly standing and sitting, often spilling his beer on my handbag, chain-smoking cigars which smelled like rotting mulch with a nice ripe afterglow of skunk, and always hogging the armrest.

Finally, when he stood up for the hundredth time, I asked him, "Would you mind?"

He looked down at me. "You got problems, lady?"

He hadn't noticed one of them, that globs of mustard from his carelessly discarded packets had stained my slacks.

"Never mind," I said.

He insisted. "Yo, lady, you got something up your skinny ass all of a sudden, or what?"

He seemed puzzled. No, moronic is a better word.

I stood up. I was relieved I was taller than he.

I know height often has its advantages.

Suddenly, someone, something somewhere inside of me said, "Yes, I do have something up my skinny ass right now. You. Stop yelling about the pinch hitter. It's strategy."

He threw a condescending look at me.

"Shut up. What the hell do broads know about baseball anyway?"

My time had arrived.

At that moment, I was overcome.

Belligerence and sarcasm had been birthed in me.

I had been following the game closely for about two years now, reading biographies and autobiographies of the players, compendiums of noteworthy seasons, the World Series and the

All-Star Games, and dozens of books and articles about the history of the game in addition to the sports sections in two newspapers every day from April to October. I even had made friends with a man named Robin Bergstrom who worked at the Elias Sports Bureau. With our unquenchable thirst for baseball, Robin and I have become very dear friends.

"Look, mister," I think I said, "baseball is unique for a lot of different reasons, pinch hitters notwithstanding."

He stood there, bending his neck off to the side, then snapped the tip of his tongue off the roof of his mouth to make that little chirping sound, tttttthhhhhh, you know, as if to say, 'Spare me,' or 'Why am I standing here listening to this?'

I insisted.

The words just flew out of my mouth.

"First of all, and I'm going to say these words nice and slow to make it easier for you to understand me, it's the only game in which the offense never touches the ball."

I was shaking. I was scared.

But then I noticed his condescending demeanor seemed to change slowly to one of interest, with a sudden tinge of astonishment.

I went on. "It's played on fields which are not consistent, they vary, they're all not the same dimensions. The one in charge of the team is called the manager, not a coach like in other team sports, and he wears the same uniform as the players do, which coaches don't."

I had him now. He was staring at me like he'd just seen the Grand Canyon for the first time, marveling at its breadth and depth.

"And," I said even more slowly, "there's no clock, nooo buzzer, noooooo bell. See the anomalies?"

Thankfully, he wasn't angry, but only dumbfounded, which finely suited the pathetic look on his face, not only because he had never thought of the game in those terms, but also because he apparently didn't know what the word *anomalies* meant.

He reached down, grabbed his stuff, and then left.

I assume he went to find another seat someplace where he didn't have to sit next to some woman who had something up her skinny ass.

I sat down, exhausted.

My mind flashed again.

I thought of Mr. Bill Kaufman, the agent from LoneStar, and the first time I had met him when he wanted to screw me and to take advantage of David's legacy.

I recall that day at the Stadium because I know that was only the second time in my entire life, literally and figuratively, that I ever had stood up to a man.

29

Sunday, January 7, 2001
Manhattan

Over the muted chatter echoing in the briefing room, Captain Tom Angola began mumbling something about the day's business and by handing out pamphlets with information about OSHA warnings of workplace environmental hazards.

Vanessa scanned hers quickly.

She whispered to herself, This place is a bad accident waiting to happen.

Then, amid the statical ruffle of papers, heavy footsteps echoed.

Heads turned.

There was silence.

Jeremy Myers had entered the briefing room, looked around, then sat down.

It was his first day back.

Tom sensed the tension. He tried his hand at humor to lighten the air. "Okay, very good. Now, don't read these, people, just memorize them."

No one laughed.

During the remainder of the briefing, Vanessa often sensed eyes upon her.

She knew they were Tony's. She still felt his anger.

She knew they were Tom's. She still felt his frustration.

She knew they were Jeremy's. She still felt his guilt.

She wondered to herself, How am I ever going to be able to do this everyday?

After the briefing, Vanessa went to the ladies' room.

Donna Lewis was leaning over the sink toward the mirror, touching her fingertip to the scar above her upper lip.

"Donna," Vanessa said with desperate frustration in her voice, "how can I do this, how can I—"

Donna turned to her. "I know, honey, it must be so difficult for you. I was watching them staring at you. Men are so strange sometimes. It's their damned eyes. Windows to their souls? No, windows to their boxer shorts. Women would be a lot better off if all of them were blind. They're eying you up and down a lot, more than usual, right?"

"Yes."

"Well, sweetie, I don't know what to say. But, maybe it's time. Even though you've only been here four or five months, maybe you need to start thinking about getting out of here and working somewhere else, doing something else."

"I have, Donna. I never really knew what pressures this job would have, every minute of every day. The training was so intense and so hard for me, but I wanted to do this, and I pushed myself because I wanted to be a part of this, part of the team, just to help people when they need it the most. But every day, every call, it's always someone's life on the line. And now with Tony and Tom and Jeremy, and everything that's happened with them, well I know I'm to blame, but I just can't do this anymore. I can't be with them here. It feels like five years, Donna." Vanessa paused, then, "I've been thinking about it. But do what?"

"I don't know. Look, you're young, you're pretty, you're smart. Do you have any skills you could use to change—"

"I can type," Vanessa said, holding up both her hands, her palms to her face, fanning her fingers, wiggling them.

Donna laughed. "Well, you've got the legs for it, sweetie."

Vanessa smiled at her.

"Thanks, Donna."

As Vanessa began washing her hands, she said, "You're right. I've been thinking a lot lately. I need a change. I need to change. I need to grow. I need to—"

"You need to get on with your life, Van. I can't really know what you've been through," Donna said, "but I see in you something different. I mean, I see in you something that I thought was in me when I was your age. I didn't do anything about it, though, and sometimes I regret it. I married Frank right out of high school, stayed home, took care of him, and raised our kids. I devoted my life to them."

Her voice slowed.

"Then, when Frank died, well, never mind. Don't misunderstand me, Van, I loved Frank and I love my kids. And yet, I often think about what my life would have been like if I hadn't married him, if I hadn't had kids," she swallowed hard, "if instead I had devoted my life to me, to me, to something else. Isn't that an awful thing to say?"

"No, Donna," Vanessa said, "it's not awful. It's honest."

"Well," Donna said, "I'm a lot older than you are and I know I don't know everything, but what I'm saying to you is, maybe you should think about what you are, what you really want to do, where you've been, where you are, and where you're going. Life's way too short, sweetie. I know. Don't let it slip away. It's time for a change, Van."

"Yes, Donna," Vanessa said, "it's time."

30

October 1991
Manhattan

$\mathcal{I}$t's been more than five years now into the "life begins at forty" mindset for me.

What has been going on since I aged across the cusp between my youthful thirties and my foreboding forties?

I carefully reviewed, analyzed, and then restructured David's Writing Fund. With the help of some pretty sharp investment analysts and brokers, really smart financial people, a steady upturn in the value of my portfolio during the late '80's, and my faithful deposits from the royalty and residual checks I still receive from David's book and the movie, *Darkness and Light*, the net worth of the fund has increased markedly and substantially. Consequently, in addition to the summer stipend salaries for public school English teachers working on their Master's degrees and their writing, I've been able to begin offering yearly sabbaticals to select applicants who wish to work on their projects for twelve months at a clip and not have to worry about putting food on their tables for themselves and their families all year long. I now oversee an endowment program valued at more than $3,000,000.

I completely renovated the two brownstones on the sides of the one I live in. The six families who are my tenants are wonderful people. In one building, there's Mr. and Mrs. Christiansen and their two little boys, Frederick and Stephen; the, what's the best way to say it nowadays, the life partners Mr. Craig and Mr. Fallon, and their boxer, Hampton; Mr. McNeil and Ms. Jackson, a lovely interracial couple; and, in the other building, Ms. Sabatello, Ms. McNally, Ms. Klarin, and Ms. Marcus, graduate students enrolled at New York University; Mr. and Mrs. Fiscella, an old-fashioned, childless Italian couple in the twilight of their years; and, Ms. Karen Caccaro, a beautiful, radiant, divorced woman with whom I've become close.

Karen's told me that after leaving her husband, she fell in love with a man who recently had divorced his wife. They had many whirlwind interludes, dating for a few years, nurturing their torrid relationship, but, alas, plans didn't materialize for either of them. They both went their separate ways. I feel so bad for her sometimes. After all, happiness is so elusive.

Anyway, I've also made some changes in my wardrobe. I've been dressing more up-to-date, more youthfully I guess one would say, shopping a lot at a small boutique on 66th Street called Small Packages, which caters to "today's" teenaged girls and young women, sizes 0 through 5. I'm tall and skinny, I always have been, and I've come to believe that the old saying, You can never be too rich or too thin, really is one of life's basic axioms, at least for women. I've come to like really short and really tight things again, and I've been told by both men and women that I still have the body and the legs for them. So, what the hell.

I travel more now. Recently, my tenant Karen Caccaro and I vacationed in Orlando for three weeks, seeing each and every Disney offering, tourist trap and novelty attraction there is to see down there. It was fun, although Karen was a lot more intent on meeting men than I was. She has something about her, the way she carries herself, an erotic and intriguing smile, and really big, beautiful blue eyes. Men were drawn to her. They just couldn't resist. She did, sometimes, though, because she's been hurt. Now, she's careful. I'm slowly learning from her what it means to be selective with men.

And there's been Robin. I met Robin Bergstrom at an art gallery in SoHo about four years ago, at a show of some third-rate artist who dabbled with uninspiring oils and maudlin acrylics trying to form a vision of something which has escaped me to this day, a western, mountains, way-out-West, animals-in-the-wild, snow-and-rocks-everywhere mélange of what seemed to me to be mediocre greeting card art as opposed to serious artistic expression. In the days and weeks after the show, Robin and I gradually became friends. He works at the Elias Sports Bureau and is a nice fit for me with my interest in professional baseball. Robin, I call him Rob, is my age, a nice looking man, funny, and extremely knowledgeable about the game. He's married with three grown children. I've met his wife Barbara and his kids a few times, and Barbara knows exactly what we do. We meet maybe twice a month for lunch, trying exotic restaurants all over the city. Our relationship is totally platonic. When he and I get together, we keep each other's baseball interests sharp and keen, we eat like pigs, and we analyze the sport in general and the Yankees in particular. It seems Barbara hates sports—opposites attract, don't they?—and she possesses a basic, bland, well-done meat-and-potatoes palate, so, in a way, I'm a nice fit for her, too. She doesn't have to talk to her husband about baseball and she doesn't have to try Thai, Vietnamese, Indian, Mexican, Japanese, Moroccan, or any other exotic cuisine.

A few times, though, I've caught myself thinking about Rob in a different way, in a different place, in a different mood, in different circumstances, but something deep inside me still makes it hard for me to tuck away my memories of David and of what we had, which is something I would have to do if anything other than small talk and steamy food ever developed between Rob and me. Although, and it pains me to write this, considering my infrequent and unrealized fantasies of being with Rob in a more personal and then in an intimate and sexual way, and my traveling with Karen and seeing how men gravitate toward her, I can imagine, sometime down the road, a really long road, I could be with a man on a more romantic level, and that such a thing might be in the cards for me someday.

Might be.

But, he's not the one.

Forgive me, but I just can't see myself with a man named Robin.

31

Monday, January 8, 2001
Hoyt Street

The phone rang at exactly one minute after noon.

Vanessa woke in her bed, then rolled over to reach for it.

"Whaaat?" she asked dreamily.

"Hey, sleepy head! You said I could call you after twelve, and after twelve it is."

"Oh, hi, Jimmy. Yes, yes it is. My alarm went off fifteen minutes ago and I don't even remember shutting it off."

"Wake up call, then," Jimmy said, blowing a kiss into the receiver.

"That's nice, baby. Here's one for you."

"Listen, Van, everything's all set on my end. How about you?" Jimmy asked.

"Yes. I told Donna and she's taking care of it for me. I'm using vacation days for Wednesday, Thursday and Friday. I'm glad we decided to make it for five days instead of four. I'm about half packed and I just need to run a few errands, which, I guess, I really should be doing right now."

Jimmy asked, "If there's anything you need at the store, I could go and get it for you, okay?"

"No, sweetie, thanks anyway. I'll do it before I go in today."

"Okay," Jimmy said. "The entire house upstate is clean,

there's four bottles of Colombard and a bottle of bourbon on the rack in the kitchen, lots of food in the fridge, gallons of seltzer and about two dozen lemons, firewood split and stacked, and fresh linens on the beds," he took a breath, "on all the beds, the skis are waxed, and—"

"Jimmy! When did you do all that?" Vanessa asked.

"Yesterday. I drove up early and stayed late. I wanted everything to be nice for you."

"You are so sweet to me, Jimmy. I would've helped you."

"No way," he said, "and you know, I don't know if I should tell you this, but I guess I will. I'm domesticated, I cook, clean, iron, do laundry, even an occasional window or two, so I just wanted this to be, well, you know—"

"Yes, I do. Thank you, sweetie."

"And," Jimmy said, his drawl sneaking in between some of his words, "I have lift tickets for us for the whole five days, and I checked the pond at the college and it's frozen solid, the green flag's up so we can ice skate, and," he took another deep, slow breath, "there's a—"

"Tell me, Jimmy, tell me," Vanessa said excitedly.

"—and there's a fantasy film retrospective at the college on Saturday."

"There's a movie theater at the college?" Vanessa asked.

"Yes, a small one, more like a super-sized auditorium. It's in the old Main Building, on the right side on the first floor. They have a really nice snack room with vending machines down there, too. Maybe we could have a nice dinner there?"

Vanessa laughed.

"I have tickets if you're interested. They have movies there every now and then, and this weekend they're featuring *Planet of the Apes* with Roddy McDowell, *Fantastic Voyage* with Raquel Welch, *Darkness and Light* with Al Pacino, and two or three others."

"That's great, Jimmy."

"Look, Vanessa," he said earnestly, "we can do all that stuff or we can do none of it. It's up to you. You decide. I just didn't want us to lack for something to do. I want you to have a wonderful time. I want you to be with me and to share some of the things which are a part of my life. I love the place upstate, I love movies, I love skiing, ice skating, sitting by the fire, eating, drinking—"

Vanessa chuckled. "I like you a lot, Jimmy Russert. We'll have a great time, I just know it. See you tomorrow, baby. Bye."

Vanessa hung up.

Choices! The man's offering me choices!

This is unbelievable, she thought.

32

March 1994
Manhattan

$\mathcal{I}$ lost David almost a quarter century ago.

Lately, I've been thinking about him more, not less, and I constantly find myself being able to recall so many things about him, the places we went, the things we did, and many of the conversations we had had during those three wonderful years we spent together upstate at our home in New Paltz.

When I'm there, I look around the rooms and see ghosts of him all about, not in the macabre or Hollywood sense, but as if he's been away from me for only a short while, maybe lecturing at a college somewhere in New England, or gathering research for a new book, or shopping in town, or just out in the garage tinkering with something.

I remember last summer, just before Labor Day. I was tidying up the house for my tenant who was to arrive in a few days, changing the linens, straightening up my messes, and organizing some things on the desk we have in the den.

I came across an old pair of David's glasses buried in the back of one of the side drawers.

I had been sitting at the desk, reaching in to grab some scraps of paper when I felt the case.

I took it out, opened it, and I stared at the glasses for what seemed like hours. I ran my fingers along the frame. I even put them on.

Everything, both up close and far away, was so blurry. I broke down then, my tears splashing on the lenses. I was overcome with knowing that David had worn these glasses almost every waking hour, and that the frame had rested on his nose and on his ears.

I know it's silly, but I felt so close to him then, turning my head from side to side, looking through the bottle-bottoms which distorted everything around the room. I composed myself, and then I wondered about all the things he must have seen through these lenses.

Then, I cried again.

In the kitchen, the cabinets were very orderly, but I decided to rearrange a few of the dishes, serving trays, cups and saucers into somewhat of a disarray so my soon-arriving tenant wouldn't think I was totally anally retentive.

I reached up on tiptoes to the top shelf and found one of David's mugs. I brought it down.

It was an oversized coffee mug which had a small, tunnel-like opening through its base, a novelty item he must have gotten from somewhere, and it was inscribed with *Practice Putting (Also Good For Coffee)*. David liked golf, more than Mark Twain, I think it was, who had said it was a good walk spoiled, but not as much as the fanatics who can't go more than two consecutive summer days without being out on the links.

I held the mug by its handle, then touched it to my lips. I kissed it.

I went into the living room. We have an old credenza made of mahogany which David had refinished, taking the doors off it and its drawers out, fashioning it into a bookcase.

I was straightening the volumes when I came across a marble composition notebook tucked in between *Bartlett's Familiar Quotations* and Edith Hamilton's *Mythology*.

It was one of David's, his means of choice when he would

write. I took it from the shelf. Its cover was creased and tattered, its spine peeling, the pages slightly jaundiced from age.

I opened it, and right away his awkward and exaggerated handwriting jumped off the page at me. I thumbed the leaves and realized it was a collection of his poems.

David never had shown me any of his poetry. He said it was his soul and that he didn't want me to see inside him that way.

I hadn't insisted.

His soul, I thought.

So, I closed the notebook.

But then, on impulse, I opened it again, fanning the pages, and then I saw a draft of a poem he had called *Yes, Your Eyes*.

In the margin, he had scribbled a date.

June 25, 1964.

That was my high school graduation day.

I read the poem.

Yes, Your Eyes

You were happy then. Yes, and so was I, I guess.
Remember? You spent the day afield and at your peak,
and then you brought to me your dream
of you and me sent from somewhere.
"Seek everything joyous from me!" you had said.
You wanted me to, with you, in bed.
And now that date of when we met
(yes, your eyes)
will be your day of fate
until the day of my goodbyes.

I remembered meeting David at the goal post after the ceremonies that day. I remembered making such a tremendous fool of myself, throwing myself at him, begging him to love me. I remembered the hurt I felt when he told me it could not be.

And now, I realize there was something there then, something he had felt for me, something he wanted, but he knew it was wrong, something neither of us had realized at the time would stay latent and asleep in both of us until our chance meeting three years later at the college when I went to meet him at his classroom in the Main Building.

Reading his poem. I was happy.

Now I know his feelings for me had begun to stir within him when I was his student and he was my teacher during those three wonderful years I sat hypnotized and desirous of him in his high school English classes.

He did like me then, he did want me then, and he did love me then.

Yes, yes, I realize it had started as prurience, lasciviousness and lust. I was a teenager and he was a married man over forty years old then.

But, in my heart of hearts, that just doesn't seem to matter to me now.

I now know something had been there, something had been in his heart for me, all those years during high school and before our talk at Barnaby's when he had told me that he needed me in his life. Something had been born, then lay dormant, and then, three years later, flourished.

Now I know he wanted me from the beginning.

I closed the notebook.

And then, I felt I had trespassed, as if I was an intruder, as if I had trudged with mud-soaked boots on a white carpet, as if I had watched two lovers during an intimate and private moment when they didn't know I was there.

I felt as if I had entered a tomb of the dead.

Why did I read his poem?

Why?

I had disobeyed him for the first time.

Against his wishes, I had opened the window to David's soul, and peeked in.

33

Tuesday, January 9, 2001
Manhattan and New Paltz

The hours crept by slowly for Vanessa, her usual eight-hour shift this day seeming like it was eight weeks.

All she could think about was that everything was ready for her trip upstate with Jimmy, their plans were made, their activities arranged, their time together coming soon.

Soon.

At last, she found herself in the firehouse locker room, hearing the voices of Donna Lewis, Tamara DeMarco, Kelly Quinn, Ricki Vargas and Melissa Elvan along the row of lockers on either side of her.

"So," Donna said, leaning toward Vanessa, "bet you're ready to fly out of here."

"Oh my, I can't wait, Donna," she said, tugging at her work shirt in haste. "Damn," she chirped, realizing a button had popped off.

Donna picked it up for her. "Take it easy, Van, he and his kisses will still be here for you if you're five minutes late, you know."

"I know, Donna, I know. I'm not meeting him now anyway. He's picking me up tomorrow at my apartment at ten, but I just want to hurry. Maybe the night will go faster if I do. And, well, I think something's going to come of this. I feel it in my heart. In my heart of hearts. I just do. I told you that he went up there Sunday to make sure everything was right and all, and then he made all these plans for us, things for us to do, and then he leaves it up to me whether I want to do them or not."

"That's great, Van," Donna said. "Well, we both know he's smitten toward you, and I know he wants to, I mean, I guess he—"

Vanessa smiled at her. "You don't have to be round-the-bush with me, Donna. He's already done it with me, okay? A couple of times."

Then Vanessa put her fingertips to her lips and opened her eyes as wide as they would go. "Lots of times!"

They laughed.

"But," Vanessa said, pulling on her turtleneck sweater, "it's not just that. Really. I keep thinking about his voice, how he talks to me, and how he listens to me, how we just hit it off at Fiore's on New Year's Eve, and then how he dropped by here to see me on Friday. I mean, the first time I met him I liked him and all, and we had fun and everything, but I didn't think I would ever see him again after that night. And then he sweeps me off my feet by inviting me upstate and making sure everything would be just so at his house, and then offering me the chance to say no or do other things."

Donna asked, "Looks like you're smitten, too?"

"I am," Vanessa said, "I really am. I mean this is so different for me. If you only knew what I've been through, what my experiences with men have been like, Donna, not just now but ever since junior high school. All they ever did was take, take, take. All they ever said was, 'Shut up, bend over, open your legs, on your knees, open your mouth,' and all I ever did was give, give, give. With him, it's the little things, like how he gets so excited when I tell him about where I grew up, where I went to school, what my family's like, all the boring stuff. He listens to me. He's interested in me and what I'm thinking. It's hard to explain, I guess."

"No, Van," Donna said, "it's not hard to explain. You just did a pretty good job of telling me. You know, if I do say so myself, I think my sense of first impressions is still pretty sharp. I liked him, too. I like him for you. You deserve this, you understand me?"

"Yes, Donna. Thanks. You're so nice to me."

Vanessa took the gold chain and pendant from the hook inside her locker. She opened the clasp of the necklace with her fingertips, then took the ends to place the necklace around her neck, carefully securing it.

"Wow," Donna said, looking at the necklace around Vanessa's neck, "this is special!"

"It is," she whispered, "it's very special."

Vanessa left the locker room, then went to her car. She started it up, revved it a few times, buckled herself in, engaged the heater switch, flipped on the lights, and then adjusted her rear view mirror. She slowly pulled out into the street, gradually accelerating, hearing the 'Vette whine a little as she shifted to second, then to third, then to fourth.

About two blocks from the firehouse, Vanessa noticed high-beam headlights flashing behind her.

At first, she ignored them.

Some moron doesn't know what the little blue light on the dashboard means, she thought.

All the way downtown, the lights behind her strobed.

She became frightened.

When she made a left onto Delancy Street, she could see the car was still following her, but during her turn its lights were temporarily out of her rear view mirror.

She now could see it was a black Cadillac.

It can't be Tony, she thought, or Jeremy, or Donna.

Pickup truck, minivan, Camry.

What kind of car does Tom drive again?

Wait, a Pontiac.

Then, Who the hell is this?

She decided to drive to the curb.

She stopped, hoping the Cadillac would keep on going. It didn't.

In her side view mirror, she saw it veer across the solid yellow line into the oncoming lane and pass by her. Then she saw it make a wide u-turn, then swerve toward her, stopping head-on in front of her, its headlights momentarily blinding her.

She heard the driver's side door open.

Oh God, she thought.

She heard the door close.

In the glare, she could define a figure walking in between the front of the Cadillac and her 'Vette, now just standing there, facing her.

Its legs were spread, its arms raised almost to its shoulders.

The headlights outlined the figure.

For a moment, it reminded her of a crucifixion.

Then, a man's voice.

"What do I have to do to get you to stop?"

Vanessa hopped out of her car.

She ran to him, embracing him.

"Jimmy, Jimmy, I was so scared. Why did you do that to me?"

"I wanted to surprise you," he said. "No, I didn't mean like that, Van. I'm sorry if I frightened you, but when I got to the firehouse Donna told me you had just left. And then I saw your car pull out so I ran back to mine and tried to flag you down."

They kissed.

"What a relief. I thought I was going to be—"

"I'm sorry. I apologize. It was stupid of me, but I didn't want you to drive all the way back to Brooklyn tonight. I thought we could leave from here."

"I can't, sweetie! All my stuff's at my apartment. The plan was you were going to pick me up there tomorrow morning at ten, remember?"

They continued to hug.

"I know, I know," Jimmy said, his voice slowing, "but I couldn't wait. You don't know how much I've been looking forward to this, Van. It's all I've been able to think about for the past few days."

Vanessa kissed him on the cheek.

"Welcome to the club," she said.

"Okay, how about this?" Jimmy asked. He kissed her forehead and squeezed her tightly. "What if I leave my car at the garage our firm has, it's not too far from here, and, well, then we could go to your place, get your stuff, and then, if you don't mind driving, or I could drive if it's okay with you, we could head on up right now, tonight?" He paused, looking into Vanessa's eyes, searching for her mood, her thoughts. "Or, we could go with what we had planned, and we could say I'm a screaming lunatic, and you can go to your place and get some sleep, and I'll spend the night at the mental health clinic, and then I'll pick you up tomorrow at ten, like we said."

Choices, Vanessa thought, always choices.

"Well," she said, "there won't be any traffic now, so why don't we drop off your car, and then head for Hoyt Street?"

He kissed her nose. "Follow me!"

At the company garage, Jimmy parked his car, then slid into Vanessa's Corvette.

"Nice, Van," he said, "nice. '77?"

"It's a '78, used to be my dad's before my mother told him to, well what she actually said to him was, 'Victor, you've got to cool your jets with this midlife crisis already, it's either me or the wheels,' and then he was going to sell it, but I gave him my sad puppy-dog look and then he gave it to me."

Soon they were driving over the Brooklyn Bridge, then heading for Hoyt Street.

Vanessa found a parking space in front of an all-night deli, a few doors down from her apartment.

They got out, Vanessa heading away from the front of her car toward her apartment, Jimmy walking straight ahead toward the deli.

"Hey, you!" Vanessa called out. "It's over here!"

"I know," Jimmy said. "Donna told me the number. I'll go in here and get us a sandwich and a soda to share on the ride, okay?"

"Sure," Vanessa said.

He's considerate, she thought.

"Do you need help carrying your stuff down?"

"Nope, it's not much. It'll take me maybe five minutes, okay?"

He's thoughtful, she thought.

"Okay, you get your things and I'll meet you here."

"Yes, Sir!" Vanessa said, saluting him.

He's so organized.

She went toward her apartment door thinking about how Jimmy always seemed to have things under control, how he plans ahead, how he must be such a wonderful attorney, always in charge, decisive, knowledgeable, but sensitive to what others are thinking.

Thirty-five minutes passed.

Vanessa had showered, dressed, did a quick inventory of her overnight bag, watered her two Swedish ivy plants in the kitchen window, then left a note on her door for Brenda.

Finally, she came out onto the sidewalk, seeing Jimmy leaning against the passenger's side door of the 'Vette.

"That was some five minutes!" he said cheerfully.

He stared at her as she walked toward him. Her hair was wet and shiny, luxuriously black. He noticed she had changed from her jeans, turtleneck sweater and sneakers to over-the-knee, black leather boots, black tights, a black mini skirt, a tight, white cardigan sweater, and her black leather bolero jacket.

"I'm sorry, baby," she said, "just a few last-minute things."

"It was worth the wait. You look stunning, Van."

"Thank you, Jimmy. Hey, wait a minute! Where's your stuff? We didn't leave it in your car, did we?"

"No, no," he said, "I have everything I need up at the house."

I'm sure you do, Vanessa said to herself.

She threw him her car keys.

"Home, James!" she said.

The ride out of the city was quick. They shared the sandwich and the soda, Vanessa holding them for him when he wanted a bite or a sip, reminding him to keep his eyes on the road and that she'd keep her eyes on the food. There was little if any traffic, and once they cleared the Bronx, the New York State Thruway was almost deserted.

They talked constantly. Vanessa rarely took her eyes off him, studying his profile as he drove, watching his lips forming the words he spoke. She placed her hands on his right knee, often gently and slowly scratching the fabric of his slacks with her fingernails.

She could smell his cologne. It was woodsy, dark, like the ground in a pine forest, masculine, yet not overpowering. She frequently found herself inhaling deeply to savor the aroma.

They turned off the Thruway at Exit 18. After passing through the toll barrier, Vanessa asked, "Is it far from here?"

"Nope," Jimmy said, "just a stone's throw." Then, "Well maybe a long stone's throw, but we'll be there in about five minutes. Five actual minutes, not thirty-five."

Vanessa laughed. "Okay, okay, I get it, I get it."

They turned onto Schreiber's Lane, then pulled into the driveway.

A thin layer of snow had draped the roof of the house like wisps of icing on a cake. All the windows were lighted.

"Yikes!" Vanessa said, "This is a big house! It's beautiful!"

"Thanks. My landlord lives here during the summers. I've been renting it from her now for the past six or seven years or so, from Labor Day to Memorial Day. Seems she wants someone here during the winters to check on things, you know, to keep it homey, lived in."

"How can you stay up here for that long every year," Vanessa wondered aloud, "I mean, don't you have to show up once in a while at your firm? It's a long commute from here to the city everyday."

They got out of the car. Jimmy laced the strap of Vanessa's overnight bag over his shoulder, then offered his hand to her. "Careful, it's still a little slippery here."

Vanessa took his hand in hers.

"Actually, Van," Jimmy said as they slowly walked toward the front door, "I'm really not in the office that much."

"Why's that?"

They took the four steps up onto the porch. Jimmy unlocked the door.

"I've been lucky," he said, "I've won a few cases which, well, you know, which were financially advantageous to me. Big cases. Now I just drop by the firm maybe one day a week to pick up my check, maybe make some calls, snoop around a little bit to make sure my associates are doing what they're supposed to be doing, and I always bring my secretary coffee. She likes Dunkin' Donuts French Vanilla."

They entered the house.

Vanessa looked around.

"This is so beautiful, Jimmy! I love the fireplace, the furniture, wow, look at all those books! It's so cozy, and tastefully appointed, I think that's the term."

"Thanks. Most of this stuff is my landlord's."

Jimmy put Vanessa's bag on a chair, helped her out of her jacket, then took off his coat.

"Welcome to New Paltz," he said.

"I'm so happy to be here with you, Jimmy," she said, leaning up into his arms, kissing him on the lips.

"You're amazing," he whispered. Then, "You need to get us some wine and some bourbon from the rack in the kitchen there, glasses are in the cabinet over the sink, and I need to get this fire going, okay?"

"Yes, Sir," she said eagerly, "on my way!"

Soon, they were settled on the couch in the living room.

The fire was snapping and hissing, its flickering tongues of yellow and red flames licking up from the burning wood, its heat slowly enveloping them.

Hours passed, but without notice. They were comfortable, warm, engaged in conversation, enjoying each other's company.

"—and then I, hey, look!" Jimmy said, pointing to the windows.

A glow had appeared.

Dawn.

"I can't believe this," Vanessa said, "we've been sitting here all night talking. The time just flew by."

"I know. Maybe we should get some sleep now. I have the lift tickets for today, but we can go anytime. Ready to turn in?"

"Yes," Vanessa said, "I'm so tired. I mean not from—"

He smiled. "I know what you mean."

Jimmy led Vanessa up the stairs.

34

October 1997
Manhattan

On a very personal level, I finally have come to comprehend what Dickens meant when he wrote about the best of times and the worst of times.

It's taken me this long, at age fifty-one, to fully understand that there are many times in our lives when the best and the worst, the good and the bad, the right and the wrong, the tragic and the wonderful, seem to juxtapose themselves at the same moment and at the same place.

Fate?

A meeting of destinies, maybe?

A few nights ago, I arranged for Karen Caccaro, one of my tenants, and Hadee Shah, my old college roommate, to meet me at Mickey Mantle's Restaurant on Central Park South.

That night, Karen came from her job as assistant curator at the Museum of Natural History, and Hadee, an interpreter for a firm downtown, from some business meetings with prospective clients on Fifth Avenue in midtown, so geographically it seemed like a good place for all of us to meet. Besides, I had never been in that restaurant, and with the Yankees' season now over, I wanted to get my last taste of the sport before the winter doldrums and baseball withdrawal set in, that tedious, torturous wait for spring training to begin in five months.

We were seated at a table, drinking, laughing, gabbing our silly heads off.

"So," Hadee said, "here we are. Three men-less women. What's the deal with that?"

"Men," Karen said, pursing her lips to drink from her wine glass, "you can't live with them, and you can't live with them."

We all laughed.

"Well," I said, munching on some warm bread, "it's been a long time for me. I know among the three of us, I hold the record. David died twenty-seven years ago."

"It's been that long?" Hadee asked. "I remember that day at the college when we were sitting there on the bench. Time just flies by."

"Yes, I know," I said. "Sometimes it seems like it was a few weeks ago, and other times it seems like—"

"Hey, girls," Karen interrupted, "who's that silver fox over there, see that guy standing by the maitre d'?"

"Yum," Hadee said, "tall, handsome, salt and pepper, nice suit, shiny shoes. What else could a girl ask for?"

The man turned and looked in our direction.

"Oh, shit," I said, "I think he heard you, Hadee."

I watched as the man walked toward us with a confident but not conceited swagger, saying hello to several patrons along the way, straightening his tie, then smiling at us. He came to our table, standing in between Karen and Hadee, directly across from me.

"Good evening, ladies. John Stahl, but I prefer Jack," he said. Then, after scanning our faces, "Bon nuit. Buenas Noches."

Then Hadee, Karen and I did some scanning.

I noticed his teeth, white and straight; his lips, a light crimson and thin; his nose, Roman but proportional to his face; his eyes, a smoky blue; and, his hair, thinning, but a wondrous mix of black with gray streaks flaring from his temples.

"Hi," Hadee said. "The English was for all of us, the French for Ursula here, and the Spanish for Karen, she's Italian but she looks sort of Spanish. Nice try at covering all the bases, Jack. But nothing for me? No Farsi?"

"I'm sorry—" he said, pausing a moment.

"Hadee."

"I'm sorry, Hadee. That's all I know, just three languages."

Karen piped up, "Hi, Jack. Karen. At your service. Oh, by the way, I'm double-jointed."

We laughed again.

I said, "Hello, Jack. Ursula Ransom."

Suffice it to say the three of us were smitten.

Jack pulled over an empty chair from the next table, sat down in between Hadee and Karen, then told our waiter to bring some champagne.

We talked for a long while, through our appetizers, our salads, our entrees, and our desserts.

Later, the waiter brought us brandy.

"I own the place," Jack told us, "there's really no direct connection to the Yankees, just a franchise, with a fee going to the Mantle family. Mickey was my boyhood hero. What better way to keep him close to me?"

"Shoots," Hadee said, looking at her watch, "I hate to be the one to say it, girls, but it's after ten already. I have to go."

"Me, too," Karen said.

"And you?" Jack asked me.

"She's staying," Hadee said, slyly winking at me. "She's independently wealthy, so she doesn't have to answer to an alarm clock in the morning."

"Ha—dee," I said, accenting the second syllable, "you're embarrassing me!"

"No she's not," Jack said, "she's just preparing us for the awkward moments you and I are going to have after she and Karen leave."

We all stood. Hadee, Karen and I hugged each other. Then Hadee and Karen hugged Jack, thanking him for the champagne and the brandy.

"And dinner is on me, ladies."

"Thanks, Jack," Karen said. Then, "Don't let this one get away, Ursula, his cologne is out of this world."

Hadee and Karen left. Jack and I remained at the table, talking until almost midnight.

I came to know that Jack and I had weathered similar storms. He's a widower, lives alone, and has no children. He many times finds himself lost in the reveries of his deceased spouse, Irene. He often is lonely for companionship, but afraid to be with someone for fear of what he thinks would be a blasphemy of sorts against Irene's memory.

We also share similar interests. He dabbles in painting, mostly acrylics of Caribbean scenery, as I dabble in writing. He occasionally volunteers his time at a homeless shelter, as I do at St. Luke's Hospital. Reading and baseball are two of his favorite hobbies. Mine, too.

I liked Jack. A lot.

But I was apprehensive.

I realized something had stirred in me, deep down, a warmth of feeling, a closeness, a simmering need to know more about Jack and to spend more time with him.

But, at the same time, I felt the silent presence of a ghost.

David's ghost.

"Look, Ursula," he said to me, "I know this is awkward for you. It's awkward for me, too. I'm confused, but I'm happy. I'm happy we met. I'm happy we talked. I think Hadee and Karen are wonderful people. And although I feel like I'm about to do something wrong, I just can't help myself. I need to say it. I need to see you again."

"Jack," I said, "I feel the same way. It's just I—"

"I know, Ursula." He paused, staring into my eyes. "Some memories are forever."

We went to the coat room. He helped me with my wool blazer. Then we held hands.

"Let's do a movie, or a show, or a museum," he said. "Let's go slow. Let's be friends. Let's—"

"I'd like that, Jack," I said, "at least I think I would."

We smiled at each other.

He leaned into my ear, kissing me quickly, lightly, then whispered, "Tomorrow, then. Lunch."

I went outside and met my driver.

On the way home, I was thinking.

Fate.

Destiny.

This surely is the best of times and the worst of times.

35

Wednesday, January 10, 2001
New Paltz

Vanessa Fernandez and Jimmy Russert were on their way back to New Paltz from a late afternoon of skiing at Hunter Mountain. Jimmy had taught her some of the basics, the snowplow to stop, what to do with the poles, how to lean into a turn, but Vanessa's city upbringing just hadn't lent itself very well to the country slopes, her wet and slightly bruised fanny a testament to her concerted efforts, but not to her success.

They pulled into the driveway.

"Thanks for taking me, Jimmy," Vanessa said.

"You're welcome, sweetie. I just wish it had been a little easier on you, that's all."

"I'm fine, just a little sore, and well, uncomfortable. But the sun and the cold and the air were so invigorating."

They entered the house. They took off their jackets.

"I'll start a fire if you'll—" Jimmy heard the answering machine beeping, "—who could that be?"

They went into the kitchen. Vanessa put her bag down on the counter, then reached to get some glasses from the cabinet above the sink as Jimmy pressed the message button.

"Maybe it's one of your many suitors," Vanessa said playfully.

A man's voice. "Van, it's me. You need to call me right now. Something's up."

Jimmy looked at Vanessa. "Looks like it's one of yours," he said.

"No, Jimmy, no. It's Jeremy Myers, he works with me. I don't have any idea what that's about, honest, maybe something at work, a manpower shortage. I really don't know. He doesn't even know the number here."

"Apparently he does," Jimmy said, with a tinge of jealousy in his voice. "Well, why don't you call him?"

"This is embarrassing for me, Jimmy. I'm sorry. I honestly don't know what's going on."

He handed her the receiver. "Call him, and find out."

Vanessa dug into her pocketbook, found her small address book, opened it, then bent its cover back the so M's were showing.

"You don't mind, Jimmy?" she asked.

"No, of course not. Really, it's okay. God forbid, maybe something happened at work."

She took the receiver, then dialed.

"Hello?"

"Jeremy, it's me, Vanessa," she said, "and this had better be good."

"Look, Van," Jeremy said quickly, "I got the number from Donna, she got it out of your locker on the back of that business card. I need to talk to you."

"Well?" she asked.

Jimmy got the glasses from the cabinet, poured some Colombard for Vanessa and some bourbon for himself, then went to the fridge for some cheese and fruit.

"Look, it's about the box. Remember? The box?" Jeremy asked.

"I remember the box. But so what?"

"You're not going to believe this, Van, but it seems that poor woman that night, when we were in the brownstone, you know what we did—"

"Yes, yes, I remember, I remember, the necklace and the box. So?"

And then it dawned on her.

"Oh, God," she screamed, "you mean Angola knows? You told him? Oh, God, we're going to be fired, Jeremy, we're going to be arrested! We're going to jail!"

She was shaking.

"No, no, of course I didn't tell him."

"Then what is it?"

Vanessa heard Jeremy beginning to take a deep breath.

"Tell me already!" she demanded.

"Stupid me. I thought there was money in that box. No money. Just papers. I finally read the pages that were inside. Every one. It's the story of her life, Van. Every three years, she wrote about something, something that happened to her, from the time she was like three or so up until—"

He stopped.

"Up until when?" Vanessa asked.

She heard him exhale slowly.

"Up until that night, probably just before she went to bed."

Jimmy stood next to Vanessa. He was confused, hearing only half the conversation. A box? A necklace? Fired? Arrested? Jail?

Vanessa started to cry. "You mean like a diary?"

A diary?

"Yes. She wrote about growing up, boys, college, her friends, her life, all in drips and drabs. Then how she loved this older guy, her teacher when she was in his classes for three years in high school, then they separated and went their own ways, then she met him again and then she lived with him and then soon after that he died, and a lot of other things after that."

"Oh, that's so sad," Vanessa said, tears streaming down her cheeks.

Seeing she was upset, Jimmy put his arm around her to

offer her comfort.

"It's freaky, Van," Jeremy said.

"What do you mean?"

"Seems she lived in that brownstone only part of the time. She had a summer house. You'll never guess where."

"Where?"

"In New Paltz. Outside of town. On Schreiber's Lane."

"Oooooohhh my God," Vanessa breathed.

"Whose house you at now?" he asked.

"Jimmy's. Jimmy Russert," she said.

"I know, but ask him who owns the place," Jeremy said slowly.

Vanessa lowered the receiver from her ear, then looked at Jimmy.

Picking up on her discomfort, Jimmy said, "I'm in the way here, Van. I'll go in the living room and get the fire going."

"No, Jimmy, it's okay. Stay here. Jimmy, who owns this house?"

"I told you. I've been renting it for the winters the past six or seven years. A wonderful woman who lives on the East Side."

"I know, I know. What's her name?"

"Ursula. Ursula Ransom. Why?"

Vanessa returned the receiver to her ear.

"I heard him," Jeremy said. "It's her."

Vanessa gasped.

"Van," Jeremy said, "I have to go now. I just wanted you to know. That poor woman. We did something wrong, Van. We never should have taken her stuff."

Jeremy Myers hung up.

Vanessa handed the receiver to Jimmy. She ran into the living room, dropped onto the couch, burying her face in her hands, sobbing.

Jimmy followed her. He sat down next to her.

"What's wrong, baby? Tell me. Trouble at work? Trouble

with the law? I'll get you out of it."

Vanessa looked at him.

"I did something wrong, terribly wrong, Jimmy. On Christmas Eve, of all days," she said in between short breaths, trying to compose herself.

"Tell me," Jimmy said softly.

"It was a fire. About two weeks ago. A terrible fire. On East 57th. Three brownstones lit up like a bonfire."

"On East 57th?" Jimmy asked. "That's where Ursula lives—"

"Lived, Jimmy, not lives," she pleaded. Then, "She died Christmas Eve. We didn't get to her fast enough. When we went in, it was all smoke and heat, flames everywhere. She died in her bed. Jeremy was carrying her out when the front wall started to collapse. We were almost trapped inside."

Jimmy bowed his head. "Jesus. She was such a wonderful woman. I adored her. Kind, gracious, good sense of humor. This is so strange, the connection between her and me, and now with the three of us. It's incredible. Fate, maybe. I don't know what to say."

"And on the way out of her bedroom," Vanessa wept, "we did a terrible thing. I took her necklace from the nightstand, and ever since that night I've kept it in my locker, I've kept it in there, telling myself it's something for me always to come back to after my shifts, something to," she reached in her sweater and pulled out the pendant so Jimmy could see it, "to cherish, and Jeremy took this wooden box from the dresser, it had a carving on it, it looked old, and I know we shouldn't have done that, but we just did. And now this."

"It's okay, it's okay. You were doing your job and then you had a weak moment. We all do sometimes. Look at it this way, you've preserved her memory in a way. Some memories are forever, you know."

"It's not okay. I feel terrible. I'm a thief. I'm guilty as sin."

Jimmy hugged her. "Please, Vanessa. Don't torture yourself over this. Would it have been better if they had been burned? Destroyed?"

"Maybe," Vanessa said, "maybe, maybe."

Jimmy wondered, "What was in the box? Her diary?"

"No," Vanessa said, "Jeremy said just sheets of paper. That night everything happened so fast, he thought at first there might be money in it, but it was locked, and I told him I didn't want to know even if there was, so he just took it, and he just told me now that she had written something every three years, the story of her life in little pieces. Why would someone do that?"

"I know why," Jimmy said.

Vanessa looked at him again, staring into his eyes, waiting for his words.

"We became close, Ursula and I. We'd have lunch together, or dinner together, always on Memorial Day weekend when I came back to the city and she was about to come up here, and then on Labor Day, when she came back to the city and I was ready to head up here. We used to laugh about it, make a joke, you know, like we were ships passing on the weekends twice a year. She'd always talk about things, what she was thinking, where she had been in her life, where she was going. She told me about David Henry, her high school teacher. She had a crush on him, like puppy love, for three years. Then after she graduated, she didn't see him again until three years later. That's when they moved in together, here, in this house. They lived here together until he died, three years after that. She once told me that that span of time, three years, was so important and so meaningful to her, how she would measure it in months, not years, how she wanted to experience that time span over and over again, to feel the days, the weeks, like signposts, and how after a while she thought she could pace the time herself if she didn't have newspapers or calendars to look at, how she—"

"That's maybe why her writing was always three years apart."

"I'm sure it is," Jimmy said.

There were several minutes of silence.

"Well, we're here now, in her house," Jimmy said, "and it seems our paths have come together at one of destiny's crossroads."

36

Sunday, December 24, 2000
Manhattan

Christmas is for children.

I remember this Eve, some forty-five years ago when I was nine years old, living in the basic cape in Hicksville.

That night, I was pacing nervously around my bedroom just before turning in, thinking about what my parents would have for me tomorrow on Christmas morning.

For weeks, I had been pestering them for a new bicycle. I knew a girl named Francine LaMonica, who lived around the corner and down a few blocks from me on Monroe Street, had a new one, a Schwinn, a gift from her parents on her birthday, which I think was November 11th or 12th. It was a beauty. I wanted one like hers, brand new, shiny, with multicolored streamers from the handle grips.

That night, I prayed.

I actually prayed.

I don't think I have since.

Of course, I knew there wasn't a Santa Claus, so I directed my words and my wishes to the only other omnipotent being I could think of. I humbly asked Him for a bicycle, presenting my case by respectfully and gently reminding Him that I had been a good girl all year, I had done well in school, I didn't harbor any ill will for or hatred toward anyone, I honor my mother and my father, I'd done my chores, and that I would be eternally grateful if my request could be granted.

That night, even though I was jittery, trembling with anticipation, and my stomach was in knots, I fell asleep quickly.

I woke Christmas morning, early. The sun was still sleeping. I ran into the living room. There were presents scattered all about the tree. The ornamental lights were strobing in the darkness. There were large boxes, small boxes, rectangles, squares, cubes and tubes.

But no two-wheeler.

I was devastated.

My parents woke, then came into the living room. We all exchanged kisses and hugs. My father sat on the couch, my mother in a chair, and I plopped down on the rug in front of the tree.

My disappointment must have been painted all over my face, but I said nothing in regard to the missing bicycle. My parents didn't, either.

I was so angry, and I was pouting.

Something inside of me wanted to scream at them. How could you do this to me?

You knew exactly what I wanted!

It's not like I didn't drop enough hints!

How could you be so mean to me?

At that moment, I saw in my parents a cold, uncaring, thoughtless, almost evil disregard toward me.

After all the gifts were opened, we went into the kitchen for breakfast.

"Joey," my mother said to my father as she was rummaging through the cabinets above the range, "where's the waffle iron? I thought we'd have waffles this morning. A special treat for us. Didn't we put it up here?"

"I don't think so, Margaret," he said, "I thought you put it downstairs in the basement cupboard. We haven't had waffles in such a long time and I'm pretty sure it's down there with—"

"Ursula, honey," she said to me, "be an angel and go

downstairs and get it, okay? I'll get the Bisquick ready while Daddy sets the table for us."

I felt like saying, Go get your own stupid waffle iron.

But, I didn't.

I dutifully went to the basement landing, flicked on the light switch, then went down the stairs. I turned to go toward the closet and—

A few minutes later, I heard my mom's voice from the kitchen, "Ursula? Ursula, honey? Are you okay? Did you find it?"

Yes, I had found it.

In front of the closet was a brand new shiny bicycle!

I was ecstatic!

It was blue, sky blue, with a black leather seat and chrome fenders. Then I saw the streamers from the handle grips.

I realized my prayer to an omnipotent being hadn't been answered.

I knew then that it was my parents.

They had listened to me.

They had answered my prayer.

I knew they loved me.

Christmas, indeed, is for children.

My father died when I was twenty-six. My mother died a little over a year ago.

All my memories of them, particularly of that day, are in my heart, always, and forever. I miss them so much.

So, what about tomorrow? What about this Christmas?

Jack and I have been dating for three years now.

There it is again. The number three.

Anyway, I've become very fond of Jack, and I've come to need him in my life.

I know he needs me, too. And, I know he loves me.

Three Christmases ago, our first, we decided to exchange just one gift. The following Christmas, two. Then, three. This morning we exchanged four.

He gave me one of his paintings, a warm, idyllic and relaxing scene of a Caribbean isle with an inviting white beach, crystal waters, magnificent palm trees, and a sailboat. He also gave me a satin nightie with cozy slippers, a treadmill with all the bells and whistles, and a beautiful 24-carat gold box chain necklace with a gold, heart-shaped pendant. We're going to have it engraved. I gave him silk pajamas, a pair of microfiber slacks, a table-top easel with some paints and some brushes, and Aramis cologne, which has become my favorite on him.

For the past few months, we've been talking about traveling together. I've become fluent in French, and Jack is, too, and so, after making the rounds to several travel agencies and checking dozens of brochures, we've decided to go to Paris, a bonus gift for both of us. We opened our other gifts this morning because we're leaving from JFK very early tomorrow, Christmas morning.

Jack's been after me to sell my houses here in the city and my farmhouse upstate. His plan is he'd sell his house, too, and then we'd buy a new place, a different place—we haven't decided where yet—and then we'd have our own home, all our ghosts left behind.

It's been thirty years for me without my David, almost twelve years for him without Irene.

I finished packing a little while ago. It's winter now also in Paris, and we want to do a lot of sightseeing, so we'll be outdoors a lot. I'm bringing along several pairs of jeans and sneakers, sweatshirts and t-shirts, mostly casual, comfortable stuff, along with some sweaters, thermals, heavy socks, waterproof boots, flannel pajamas, and a scarf and gloves.

Jack suggested I bring some, well, some sexy stuff, too, so I've got some short skirts and tight tops which I bought at Small Packages, that store I love because the clothes there flatter me, even though they're really designed for much younger women, and also some high heels, and some tap pants and lacy camisoles to go to bed when Jack and I—never mind—and what I think is a stunning black chemise dress with spaghetti straps and a really high slit on one side, which fits me like a glove, and which, if I had a teenaged daughter, everyone would think it was hers. I also packed lots of nice panties and matching bras, and, of course, stockings and garters.

Jack says I still have the body and the legs for those kinds of things, and my modesty aside, I think I still do, too.

Tall and skinny.

I always have been.

I am what I am.

Jack at first suggested, then later insisted on the sexy stuff.

Men.

Underwear is magic.

So, what the hell.

I've made love to Jack many times. He's wonderful. I know comparisons shouldn't be made, I mean, after all, each of us makes love in signature ways, but I can't help it. He's not as demanding of, or dominating or bossy to me in bed as David was, he's not into spanking me as much, although we've fooled around a few times with that, and he's not one for tying me up and then forcing himself on me like David often did, but, all things considered, he surely knows what to do and how to do it, when, metaphorically speaking, he ices my cupcake.

Jack is taller than I am, David was shorter, and he's very strong. His hands always are slow and tender on my body, and, well, when he delivers himself to me between my legs, I feel it. I really feel it, if you know what I mean. He's very oral, and I am, too, and the magic and the music we make together is very pleasing and exciting for both of us.

I guess it's true that in the end all the love you take is equal to the love you make.

A little while ago, Hadee Shah called. She's been my best friend for more than thirty years. She works hard, gets by, and is a very proud woman. For decades she has refused to accept money from me. I've been very fortunate in that regard, the checks still coming in from David's book, *Rivers of Whispers, Stories of Knowing*, and the movie, *Darkness and Light*. I had bought a spacious loft in Tribeca about fifteen years ago, had it renovated, and I thought I would offer it to Hadee as a place for her to live in, rent-free, rather than to keep on trying to give her money outright. She reluctantly but graciously accepted, and she's been living there ever since.

And I buy her a new car every three years, she's partial to Hondas, so I've arranged with the dealership that when it's time, she'll come in, turn in the old one, then pick out a new one, any model she wants, and then they send the bill to me.

For her birthday, Christmas, and holidays, I give her gift certificates, which I wrap inside boxes of varying sizes, to as many stores as I can think of, usually Cartier, Bloomingdales, Lord and Taylor, Macy's, Abercrombie and Fitch, about eight or nine local boutiques and specialty shops, Barnes and Noble, Victoria's Secret, and sometimes even Sears, Home Depot, Old Navy, and Wal-Mart.

This year, I have fifteen different certificates for her, totaling fifteen thousand dollars.

I want to do this for her.

It gives me pleasure to do this for her, to see her happy.

Christmas is for adults, too.

Hadee is in California now, visiting her two sisters for the holidays, one in San Diego, the other in Woodland Hills. We've decided to meet after the New Year, when she's back in the city, and after Jack and I return from Europe. We've set aside the weekend of January 13th, at which time we'll have a belated Christmas and exchange gifts.

It's cold here now, light snow is starting to fall, and the wind's picking up.

I'm going to take a shower now. Be back in a few minutes.

There, that's better.

I'm looking forward to our trip to Europe and to the New Year, the new millennium.

The end of something, the beginning of something.

Transition.

I've made a preliminary list of some resolutions, observations, and desires which I've been mulling over for the past few days. I need to refine it, but I'm thinking along these lines.

I want to expand David's Writers Fund to offer more and larger stipends and sabbaticals, particularly to aspiring writers.

I want to meet Hadee more often for lunch or dinner, or just to go shopping with her, maybe to see a movie or go to a concert, take in a show or browse a museum, and to have her over more frequently for some drinks, some food and some conversation.

I want to increase my volunteer time at St. Luke's Hospital across town, maybe to do more than just the usual information desk stuff. I'm thinking I'd like to work on the Maternity Floor in some capacity, to try to help out with the little ones, their voyages just begun.

And I'm going to marry Jack.

There, I've written it.

Does that mean it surely will come to pass?

Last weekend, he and I snuggled in because the weather was so cold and ornery. We rented some movies. I especially enjoyed *The Great Gatsby*, with Mia Farrow, Bruce Dern and Sam Waterston. I loved the story, the sleepy aura of the film, and I'm thinking maybe it would be fun to drive an antique car. Maybe I'll ask Jack to help me find an old LaSalle or a Packard.

I want to try to track down old friends and acquaintances with whom I've lost touch.

I still remember Valerie Claremont from elementary school; Francine LaMonica, Lynn Rankle and Gloria Mason—my young-stuff heartbreaker buddies—and Bobby Titus from junior high school; and, Curtis Ralls and Danny Ruiz from high school.

In my mind's eye, I can see red-headed Sherry O'Shea, busty Roseanne Abruzzi, the insatiable one, Dean Young, and the serenading Dennises from college.

What about David's agent, William Kaufman, is he still at LoneStar?

And then there was Marianne Zahn, my French I and French II friend; those two little adorable girls on Palentine Place, just down from my farmhouse; and, Robin Bergstrom, the baseball nut.

Where are they all now?

What have they experienced all these years?

Will any of our paths ever meet again?

David had written about the steel design of crossroad destiny. Is there really such a thing?

I'm thinking I need to see less of Karen Caccaro, my tenant. Don't get me wrong, I love her as a friend. She's a wonderful person. But, there's this streak in her. She's so naughty, and such a bad influence on me. She's already taken me to my first Chippendales extravaganza, and, thanks to her, I've seen about a dozen porno movies of just about everything you can imagine.

When we go out for some drinks or to dinner, she sometimes forgets to be careful and it always seems she's on the prowl. Yet, most times she is selective, but prowling nonetheless.

I still laugh when she says, "A little rebellion every now and then is a good thing, Ursula, Thomas Jefferson said that, and you know how much I like guys named Thomas, Tom, Jeff, Sonny—", and then she keeps adding a dozen or so of other men's names on and on and on.

It's just I'm serious with Jack now. I don't need any temptations. But, I haven't forgotten it was Karen, three years ago, who pointed Jack out to Hadee and me at Mickey Mantle's.

Maybe Mr. Jefferson and Karen are right.

Maybe a little rebellion is a good thing, every now and then.

I'm tired.

It's late.

Everything is ready for tomorrow.

I need to finish with this, and then tuck it into my writing box.

Oh David, David, another three years has passed.

I still love you with all my heart.

I still miss you so much.

Ooops, I almost forgot. I need to water the Swedish ivy I have by my window.

My alarm is set for 4:30, so I will go to bed now.

Maybe I'll dream.

Maybe I'll dream of what has been.

Or, better yet, of what will be.

Oh, a few more things for my list.

I want to do more, to see more, to experience more, and to learn more.

I want to make the most of whatever time I have left.